J
D 91s

-13, 838=
Duncan, Lois

Stranger with my
face

DATE			

© THE BAKER & TAYLOR CO.

STRANGER
WITH MY
FACE

by

Lois Duncan

Little, Brown and Company   Boston   Toronto

Fourth Printing

Library of Congress Cataloging in Publication Data

Duncan, Lois, 1934–
    Stranger with my face.

    Summary: A seventeen-year-old senses she is being spied on and probably impersonated, but when she discovers what actually is occurring, it is more unbelievable than she ever imagined.
    [1. Astral projection — Fiction. 2. Twins — Fiction] I. Title.
PZ7.D9117St   [Fic]   81–8299
ISBN 0–316–19551–0   AACR2

MV
*Published simultaneously in Canada
by Little, Brown & Company (Canada) Limited*

PRINTED IN THE UNITED STATES OF AMERICA

For David and Maria Martin
Mary Ann, Johanna and Elizabeth

CHAPTER 1

My name is Laurie Stratton. I am seventeen years old, and I live at the Cliff House on the northern tip of Brighton Island.

My parents moved here with me when I was four. My father is a science fiction writer, and my mother is an artist, so this out-of-the-mainstream existence suits them well. They bought this house from the descendants of the Brighton family, who at one time owned the island, and had it remodeled to fit their needs. Except for an occasional trip down to the village for groceries and mail, they seldom leave.

"Why go back to the rat race on the mainland," asks Dad, "when we have everything we need right here?"

There was a time when I, too, loved the Cliff House. It is perched on a ledge of rock that hangs out over the ocean, and from the balcony off my bedroom I can look out into forever. In the summer the skies are such a brilliant blue that they seem to have been painted on cardboard, and the water varies from light blue to dark blue, to aqua, to emerald green. The island is fun in the summer. The cottages at the south end fill up with vacationers, and the

Yacht Club has sailing races, and the Tennis Club has tournaments, and young men from Harvard and Yale and Princeton come swarming out from the mainland to compete for jobs as lifeguards. The Brighton Inn imports live music on the weekends, so there is a place for dancing, and the roads are filled with cyclists, and the beaches with picnickers, and the warm, sweet air with the sound of laughter and the smell of suntan oil.

In the winter the scene changes. The gray moves in, and with it, the cold. We have the place to ourselves then — my family and I, and the people in the village.

It's the villagers who gave our home its name. From the village you can look across the inlet and see it hanging out against the sky like an extension of the cliff on which it stands. The Brightons designed the house so that every room, no matter how small, has a window overlooking the sea. My mother's studio is at the top of the house, angled so that it is flooded with north light, and my father's office is downstairs off the kitchen. On the middle level there is a huge, heavy-beamed living room with a stone fireplace at the far end, and the three bedrooms climb the side of the house like stair steps, fitting the curve of the cliff. The topmost room is mine — then comes my parents' — and the third, which was originally to be a guest room for agents and editors who come out from New York — belongs to my younger brother and sister.

"If we had expected them, we would have made better arrangements," says my mother with a laugh, for I was supposed to have been an only child.

So, I live at the Cliff House with my parents, and with my brother, Neal, who is eleven, and my sister, Megan, who is eight.

And with someone else.

It is a long time since I have seen her, but I know she is here. In bed at night, above the sound of the surf on the rocks beneath my window, I hear very faintly the rustle of her passage down the hall. She moves softly, but I can hear, for I am used to the sound of her.

She pauses outside my door.

In my dreams I hear her voice. But, are they dreams? Or in the months since I saw her last has her voice become so slight that this is the only way she can reach me?

I blame you, she whispers. *Only you.*

I am not afraid of her any longer, but her presence here disturbs me. Even the beauty of the ocean is no solace. I stand at the window and stare out at the sun-dappled waves of the summer sea, and I brace myself as though against an icy wind.

My parents worry about me. They don't understand what has happened. Of the three people I could talk to, two are gone, and the third is very young.

I, too, will soon be leaving. That is why I am writing this. When I go I want to leave it all behind me — Cliff House, my memories and *her.* To do that, though, I first must pour the story from my mind into another vehicle.

I do not have my father's talent in writing. That went to Megan, just as my mother's artistic talent went to Neal. But since there is no one here to whom I can really talk, I have no choice but to set my tale on paper.

I hope I can be finished before September. . . .

. . . September. That was the beginning. September a year ago.

I awoke that particular morning with a question in my mind — Am I going to make it?

I lay there for a while, considering, almost afraid to test myself. Then, very slowly, I sat up. Nothing happened. I swung my legs over the side of the bed and hoisted myself gingerly to my feet.

Still, nothing. The room remained stable. My stomach didn't leap and lurch. My mouth tasted normal.

So, Mother had been right after all, and the dreadful bout the day before had been nothing more than one of those twenty-four-hour viruses! It was over. I was well. I would be able to start school.

I crossed the room, wobbling a little with that leftover weakness that always follows a round of stomach flu, and went out onto the balcony. It was like stepping into a bath of golden light; the sunlight seemed to be pouring in from every direction. Overhead the sky was a radiant, piercing blue, and the salt breeze still smelled like summer. The water was so calm and clear I felt as though I could look straight down through it to the sand floor below.

How impossible that fall was officially here!

In every girl's life, I guess, there must be one special summer that is a turning point, a time of stretching and reaching and blossoming out and leaving childhood behind. This was the summer that had happened to me. The year before, I had been awkward and gawky, all pointed knees and sharp elbows and bony rib cage, hiding my shyness behind a book while girls like Natalie Coleson and Darlene Briggs wriggled around in their bikinis and got boys to buy them Cokes and rub them with baby oil.

This summer it had all been different. The first day I

walked out onto the beach, clutching my book and my beach towel, I had heard a wolf whistle.

At first I didn't believe it was meant for me.

Then somebody called, "Hey, Laurie!" and I turned to see Darlene's boyfriend, Blane Savage, grinning at me. Next to him, Gordon Ahearn, who had been sprawled flat, soaking up sun, lifted his head to see what was going on.

"Hey, come on over here!" Blane called.

Slowly I walked over to stand in front of them. I was bewildered by the summons. I had been seeing Blane all year long in school, and he'd hardly bothered to speak to me.

"What do you want?" I asked.

"Just to say 'hi,'" Blane said. His shoulders were white and freckled, and he looked a lot less handsome in swim shorts than he did when fully dressed.

With Gordon, it was another thing entirely. His lean, well-muscled body seemed to keep a year-round tan. He shoved a lock of blond hair back from his face and regarded me quizzically.

"Is that a new swimsuit?"

I shook my head. "It's the same one I had last year."

"Well, something's sure different," he said approvingly. "Why don't you set up camp and stay awhile? Want some lotion?"

"No, thanks," I told him. "I never burn."

Over by the base of the lifeguard tower, Natalie Coleson was talking and laughing with a bunch of the college kids who had come over from the mainland on the ferry. Natalie had been Gordon's prom date. She was very pretty and popular, but I noticed that she had gained some weight over the winter. She was pretending to be caught up in conversation, but her eyes kept flicking in my direction.

I glanced down at my own flat stomach (overweight has never been one of my problems) and felt a sudden amazing surge of self-confidence. It was a new feeling for me to like the looks of myself and to realize that other people did too.

Carefully I spread my towel out on the sand next to Gordon's and lowered myself onto it. The sun felt grand on my back and shoulders.

"Feel like a Coke?" Gordon asked me.

I never did get around to doing any reading. I hardly picked up a book again that summer, what with all the swimming and sailing, and dances and beach parties and moonlight walks by the ocean.

I got my first kiss. Actually, that came quickly. Gordon wasn't a guy for game playing.

"You've got a sweet mouth," he told me on our first date, "and I'm going to do something about it."

He had a nice mouth too. And beautiful, sea green eyes, a strong face, and soft hair that kept getting lighter and lighter under the summer sun until it became the unreal color of corn silk.

Going with Gordon automatically made me a part of the crowd he ran with — Darlene and Blane, Natalie, Tommy Burbank, Rennie and Mary Beth Ziegler, and the various others who came and went as the in-group changed boy- and girlfriends. At first the girls were cool to me out of loyalty to Natalie. Soon, though, she zeroed in on one of the summer vacationers — Clyde Something-or-Other — and that eased the tension. Eventually she and I got to be pretty good friends. Or so I thought.

That was one reason I felt bad about missing the party.

Natalie's father owned the Brighton Inn, and Nat had talked him into letting her throw an end-of-the-summer party there. Everybody was excited about it, especially the girls, because it would give us a chance to dress up. There weren't many such occasions, since on the island everybody dressed casually for everything. I even got Mother to take me shopping on the mainland for a long dress and matching high-heeled sandals.

And then I got sick.

The flu hit suddenly, and it knocked me out completely. It was crazy; that morning I was feeling great, and by midafternoon I was sure I was going to die. I threw up everything I'd had to eat all day, and went in and fell onto the bed and didn't move again for hours. Along about five I got myself up long enough to stagger to the phone and call to tell Gordon that I wouldn't be going to the party. He wasn't home, so I left the message with his mother, who was sweet and sympathetic.

"That's such a shame, Laurie," she said. "I know it won't be nearly as much fun for Gordon if you're not there."

I hadn't thought about Gordon's going without me. If things had been reversed, I would certainly not have gone to a dinner-dance while he lay on his deathbed. At the same time, confronting the situation logically, it was silly to expect him to miss the final get-together of the season.

"Tell him I'm really sorry," I said, and then had to practically throw the receiver back on the hook as a wave of nausea came sweeping over me. Mother found me in the bathroom and put me back to bed. I fully expected to stay there until Christmas.

Which was why I was so amazed now, just one day later, at how good I felt. I drew in a final long breath of sunny air and left the balcony to get dressed.

"Are you sure you feel well enough for school?" Mother asked me worriedly as I came into the kitchen. "The first day can't be all that important, and you need to get your strength back."

"I feel fine," I told her.

Neal and Megan were seated at the kitchen table, licking the sugar off their cinnamon toast and messing around with their cereal. I had to look at them twice to be sure I knew them. All summer they had run around barefoot in swimsuits or cutoffs with their hair sticky with salt and their arms and legs plastered with grains of sand. Now they were neatly dressed in their brand-new school clothes, and Megan even had her hair curled.

"Laurie doesn't want to miss the ferry ride," she announced knowingly. "She's afraid some other girl will sit with Gordon."

As there is no school on the island, the resident kids commute to the mainland by ferry during the good weather. It's a forty-minute ride each way, and both the elementary and high schools are within walking distance of the landing. The ferry ride was fun, and as usual when she made her smug, precocious remarks, Meg was right. I did want to make the ride with Gordon. The year before, I had been one of the loners, sitting with Neal or Megan, or standing at the rail by myself or with somebody like Jeff Rankin, pretending it didn't matter that the "in" group was bunched together on the bow, laughing and joking around, oblivious to my existence.

This year it would be different. I had a place now, an

identity. I was "Laurie Stratton, Gordon Ahearn's girl," and I would be there on the bow with the others, Gordon's arm tossed casually around my shoulders as we shared the sea wind and the blowing flecks of spray.

"I feel just fine," I said again to Mother, and to prove it I ate some breakfast — not a lot, but a few bites of toast and some coffee. And then the children and I set off for the ferry landing a half mile away.

The moment we were out the door, Neal took off like a bullet and was gone, streaking down the Beach Road and disappearing around a curve. Neal never walks anywhere if he can run. Meg is strong, but fat; and I am thin, but lazy, so we just sort of jogged along together, enjoying the morning, knowing that even if we were a few minutes late Neal would make them wait for us.

When we came around the bend in the road, we could see the crowd already assembled at the landing. Rennie and Mary Beth were always there early, because their dad ran the ferry, and there was a bunch of younger kids running around, waving notebooks and lunch pails and pretending to try to shove each other into the water. Jeff Rankin was standing by himself over by the seawall. And I saw Darlene and Blane. Then, a little beyond them, I saw Gordon talking with Natalie.

I raised my hand and waved.

Darlene waved back at me, but it was an odd sort of gesture. She raised her hand halfway, then glanced at the others and slowly lowered it again. Gordon did not seem to see me, which was strange because he was looking right at me.

I slowed my pace, and Meg trotted on ahead of me, glancing back over her shoulder.

9

"You coming, Laurie?" she called.

"Yes," I told her.

Something was the matter. I could feel the vibrations of hostility stretching to meet me. My apprehension mounted as I drew nearer, and I found myself walking more and more slowly.

"Hello," I said as casually as I could when I came up to them. "What's with everybody anyway, the back-to-school blues?"

No one smiled, or even tried to. There was a moment of silence.

Then Natalie said, "You missed a good time last night. It really turned out to be a pretty great party."

"I'm sure it was," I said. "I felt awful canceling out on you. You wouldn't have wanted me, though, in the condition I was in."

"You seem okay this morning," Gordon said without preluding the statement with a greeting.

"I am," I told him. "It's like a miracle."

"It seems that way. When did it occur?"

"When did *what* occur?" I glanced in bewilderment from one unfriendly face to another. "Say, what's going on here? Let me in on the secret, will you?"

"The miracle," Gordon said. "When did it occur? Pretty quickly after you called my mother?"

"Look, Laurie," Natalie said, "you can cut out the act before it gets any more embarrassing than it already is. We know you weren't sick."

"What do you mean by that?"

"Just that. We know you're lying. That was ten bucks' worth of lobster dinner you cost my dad. If you didn't want to come, you could have said so in the first place."

"I don't know what you're talking about." I turned to Darlene. "What *is* she talking about?"

"It's not like it was a cookout or something, Laurie." Darlene's soft little voice was gently accusing. "This was a formal party. Nat's folks had gone to all kinds of trouble getting things set up with a band and all that wonderful food."

"If I'd known you didn't want to come, I would have asked someone in your place," Natalie told me. Her pretty, heart-shaped face was flushed with anger.

"Where are you getting this stuff about my 'not wanting' to come?" I was beginning to get angry myself. "What choice did I have? People don't get sick because they want to. I suppose you think it's my idea of fun to lie there in bed when all the rest of you are out partying!"

"Come off it, Laurie," Gordon said. "You weren't at home in bed any more than I was."

"I had flu," I said. "If you don't believe me —"

"I don't." His voice was flat and hard. "Because I saw you."

"You — *what?*"

"During the band intermission, I went outside to get some air. The moon was bright, and I saw you on the beach."

"Gordon, you've got to be crazy!" I stared at him incredulously. "I never left the house last night. You can ask my parents."

"I don't need to ask anybody. I *saw* you. Now, you answer me something — who was it you were meeting there? And don't try to tell me 'nobody,' because I'm not going to buy it. It was one of the summer guys, wasn't it? Which one — that dude from Princeton? Or that one with the beard who's been giving you the eye at the Tennis Club?"

He was furious. I had never seen Gordon so livid. His jaw was set, and his eyes had narrowed to slits of glimmering green.

Mr. Ziegler gave the boat whistle a toot, and I realized suddenly that we were the only ones who hadn't boarded.

"I won't even try to answer that," I said with as much dignity as I could muster. "There isn't any answer. I was home, sick in bed. Period. If you saw somebody on the beach, it wasn't me."

For a moment nobody spoke.

Then Natalie said quietly, "That's not true. I was there with Gordon. We both of us saw you. There's no way in the world it could have been anyone else."

CHAPTER 2

IT WAS A LONG, STRANGE DAY.

There were all the usual things that have to be done at the start of a new school year. I went to the office for my locker assignment, filled out registration forms, and located my new classrooms.

People I hadn't seen since the previous spring greeted me in the halls, and I smiled, said friendly things, and gave appropriate answers to routine questions.

"No, we didn't go anywhere special for vacation. Did you?"

"Oh — I swam a lot and played some tennis and just generally lazed around. What did *you* do?"

"Oh — thanks. It would be strange, though, if I *didn't* get a tan, living on the island."

And all the while, beneath the surface, I was seething. How could Gordon have had the nerve to accuse me with such certainty of something I told him I did not do? "I saw you," he had insisted, not just once but several times, without a hint of doubt in his voice. And Natalie had confirmed it. "We both of us saw you" — when I had not been there to be seen. My denial had counted for nothing. They had not believed me. Natalie had actually come right out and told me, "We know you're lying."

And what had Gordon and Natalie been doing out on the beach together anyway? That question occurred to me at midmorning when I was standing in line at the book room. Natalie was supposed to have been with Clyde, her date for the evening, not out strolling around in the moonlight with *my* boyfriend! Here Gordon was, acting so furious about something that had not happened, when I was the one who had a right to be upset and angry.

I collected my books and took them to my locker. My new lockermate was a tall, freckled girl named Helen Tuttle who had just transferred from a high school in the Southwest. It turned out we had the same split period for English, so we ended up eating lunch together in the cafeteria. Darlene and Mary Beth Ziegler came in soon after we did, but they never glanced in my direction. They went through the line and took their trays to a table at the far end of the room, and before long Blane and Tommy Burbank and some of the other island kids joined them there.

I had a ham sandwich and a Coke for lunch, and they went down perfectly. I almost wished they hadn't. If I had been sick right there in the lunchroom, Blane or somebody would surely have told Gordon, and it would have given credibility to my story of having been ill the night before.

Helen must have noticed my mind wasn't on our conversation, because she followed the direction of my gaze and asked, "Who are you looking at?"

"Oh, just some kids who live out near where I do," I told her. "They're a sort of clique."

"I guess you find those everywhere," Helen said lightly. I

was tempted to tell her I had been part of that clique only the day before, but I decided against it. I was too confused by the situation to explain it properly to somebody I had only just met.

When school let out, I held back a little and let the others start for the pier without me. I'd been snubbed soundly enough that morning without inviting it again. In the process of waiting for them to widen the gap between us, I dawdled too long and finally had to run the last fifty yards or so in order to make the boat. I clambered on board just as they were casting off, and, as luck would have it, grabbed a nearby arm for balance, and the arm happened to belong to Gordon.

"Excuse me," I said coldly, removing my hand as quickly as possible.

"You're excused," he said, and then added in a low voice, "Look, Laurie, I've had time to cool down some. You come clean with me, and I'm willing to listen to your side of the story. What were you doing out there —"

"What a coincidence!" I snapped back, interrupting him in midsentence. "That's exactly the question I had for you. What were you and Nat doing wandering around on the beach together when she was supposed to be hostessing a party?"

I didn't wait for an answer. Instead, I shoved my way past him and climbed the ladder to the narrow upper deck, which was where my brother Neal always liked to ride. When I reached it, I remembered that the elementary school operated on an abbreviated first-day schedule and the younger children had undoubtedly gone back on the noon ferry. Having made the trip up, however, I certainly was not going to turn around and go straight back down again, as though I were disappointed that Gordon had not chased after me, so I made my way along the catwalk to the small seat that overlooked the bow.

Jeff Rankin was already planted there, reading a paperback.

He acknowledged my arrival in his usual ungracious manner. "How come you're not downstairs with the party bunch? Did you have a fight with the boyfriend?"

"That's putting it mildly," I said, sitting down beside him. Jeff's abrasiveness didn't bother me. I figured he was entitled to it; I knew that if I were in his place, I'd hate everybody in the world.

Mr. Rankin had moved to Brighton Island four years before to open a shellcraft shop, and Jeff, who lived with his divorced mother somewhere in northern New York State, had started spending summers with his father. He was fourteen that first year, with the sort of dark, flashy good looks that should by rights have belonged to someone much older. The second summer he came, he had a motor bike, and there was always some squealing girl sitting on it behind him with her arms wrapped around his waist and her chin on his shoulder. Sometimes her hair was dark and sometimes blond and sometimes red, but it was always long and shiny, flying out behind them like the tail of a comet as they went roaring down the road.

I turned fourteen myself that year — a skinny, flat-chested fourteen — and I dreamed at night about what it would be like to be one of those girls.

The island guys were all jealous of Jeff that summer, although they wouldn't admit it. There was a lot of talk about how wild he was, and rumor had it that several fathers among the vacationers complained to Mr. Rankin about his son's activities with their daughters. The girls themselves were never heard to complain, and since most of them were older than he was, I thought they should have been able to take care of themselves. As it happened, it was a good thing Jeff did have that summer, because halfway through the next one a can of lighter fluid exploded and burned off half his face.

They took him to the mainland by helicopter. The kids who were at the cookout when the accident occurred — Rennie Ziegler was one of them — described the details to everyone who would listen.

"The medics were shaking their heads when they put him on the stretcher," Rennie said. "He kept making these gurgling noises like he was trying to scream and couldn't. There's no way he could live after that — I swear it."

Jeff did live. They even managed to save his eyes, thanks to the fact that he had been wearing sunglasses. He came back to the island at Christmas, but nobody saw him; Mr. Rankin explained that he wasn't strong enough yet for any visiting. Soon after that he went back to the hospital for an operation. The next summer he returned to the island, this time to stay. The left side of his face was fine. If you saw him at a certain angle, you'd have thought he was the best-looking guy you'd ever seen. If you saw him from the right, you had to stop and swallow hard. That side of his face was welted and purple with the eye half closed and the mouth pulled up at the corner like a Halloween mask. All the kids tried to be nice to him and act like there was nothing wrong with the way he looked, but he made it clear that he didn't appreciate their efforts. He stayed in the house most of the time; his dad said he was supposed to stay out of the sun. When September came, we thought he'd go back to New York, but he started school with the rest of us. He had lost a year, which put him in my grade. We none of us knew why he had decided to live on the island instead of with his mother, and nobody wanted to ask him.

As Rennie put it, "You can't talk to somebody who's got his hackles up all the time. His personality's gotten just as messed up as his face."

Now, as I settled myself on the bench beside him, I didn't really care what his personality was like. I was too absorbed in my own anger.

"To say I've 'had a fight' with Gordon is putting it mildly," I said. "I don't care if I never see him again. You know that party Nat Coleson threw last night?" Immediately, I could have cut my tongue out. You don't discuss parties with people who aren't invited.

"Nope," Jeff said, not making things any easier.

"Well — she had one," I continued lamely. "At the Inn. I didn't go."

"Then you must have been sick," Jeff commented.

"As a matter of fact, I was. Which is what this whole thing is about." Despite my intentions, the words came pouring out of me. I knew there was no reason for Jeff to be interested, but he was there next to me, a captive audience, and I had to talk with somebody or I'd burst. "Gordon won't believe me," I told him. "He swears he saw me out on the beach during intermission. He's accused me of pretending to be sick so I could go sneaking off with somebody else."

"Gordon Ahearn thinks that?" There was a note of sarcasm in Jeff's voice. "How could he? Everybody knows he's got you on a string."

"He does not!" I exclaimed.

"Well, sure he does. You're as faithful as a puppy dog. He snaps his fingers, and you jump. That's how it's always been with Ahearn's girlfriends."

"You don't know one thing about my relationship with Gordon," I said irritably. "I do what I want to do. Nobody runs my life for me."

"Then you *were* there making out with some other guy?"

"No, I wasn't!" I exploded. "I just told you, I was home sick in bed. Gordon didn't see me on the beach."

"Then why does he say he did?" Jeff asked reasonably.

"I don't know." I paused, and then threw out the final piece of information. "It's not just Gordon. Natalie was there too. They both say they saw me."

"So there are three possibilities."

"Like what?"

"Number one — you were there and won't admit it. Number two — you weren't there, and Gordon and Nat are in cahoots."

"And number three?"

"They saw somebody who looks exactly like you."

Hearing it presented that way, there wasn't much I could do except nod. Those were, indeed, the only three alternatives.

"But why would they make up a story like that?" I asked in bewilderment.

"That's a good question. *You* tell *me*."

"There isn't any reason."

"So where does that leave you?"

"With — number three. That there was someone who looks like me on the beach last night. But Gordon says there was bright moonlight. It's hard to believe he and Nat would both be fooled, especially when they weren't expecting me to be there."

"You've got a strange sort of looks," Jeff said.

"Well, thanks a lot!"

He didn't apologize — not that I had expected him to. He turned and looked at me appraisingly. It was always a shock to have Jeff look at you straight on like that, because the two sides of his face were so different. I'd been sitting on his good side, so when he turned toward me I had to adjust for a second.

He studied me a moment, then shook his head.

"No, there aren't many people around here who look like you," he said.

He reopened the book, which had fallen shut on his lap, and it was apparent that he meant for our conversation to be over.

The whole way to the island I brooded over his comment. Rude as it was, it was true. I didn't have the sort of looks you found just everywhere. Gordon kidded sometimes that I could be part Indian with my dark coloring, high cheekbones and almond eyes. "Bedroom eyes," he called them, meaning they were sexy. My father referred to them as "alien" because they were the same shape as the eyes he gave to the maidens from other worlds in his novels. When I looked at my parents — both of them so fair — and at Neal and Meg with their light blue eyes and freckled noses, I wondered sometimes how I had managed to be born into such a family.

So, what did it all add up to? That there was another girl who had "strange looks" also? That she was living on Brighton Island and I'd never run into her? That seemed impossible. In the summer, of course, there was an influx of tourists, but few stayed on into September, especially those with school-age children. Rennie worked the ferry with his father during the summer months, and he made it his business to inspect the girls. If there had been one who could have been my identical twin, he would have mentioned it, if only to tease me.

Which brought me back to Jeff's proposition number two — that Gordon and Natalie had invented the girl-on-the-beach story. But why would they do such a thing? What purpose would it serve? If Gordon wanted to break off with me, there were plenty of simpler ways to go about it, and Natalie wouldn't have to be involved at all.

"It has to be that they lied," I said to Jeff as we descended the ladder to the main deck. "But it doesn't make any sense."

"Don't lose any sleep over it," he muttered. "Ahearn's not worth it."

At any other time I would have resented the statement. Now I wanted to believe it was true.

We deboarded at the landing and walked side by side along the pier to the road.

"See you tomorrow," I said, and Jeff mumbled something undiscernible, apparently sorry he had devoted so much of his valuable time to me.

He headed off southward toward the village and I in the opposite direction toward the point. The first short segment of the road was cut off from the water by dunes and sea oats, and the air was still and hot as though the remnants of summer were trapped there waiting for release. When I reached the curve, however, the salt breeze struck me full in the face, and with it came the smell of seaweed and of the surf as it swirled around the rocks. Up ahead, perched precariously on its ledge, Cliff House was silhouetted against the glare of the afternoon sun. The slanted rays glanced off the windows of my mother's studio with such brilliance the whole upper story seemed formed of dancing rainbows. I wondered how she could work, caught in the turbulence of such many-shafted light. Beneath this sparkling crown, the rest of the house seemed no more than a one-dimensional, construction-paper cutout glued to the sky.

Then suddenly I had the feeling that I was being followed. I glanced quickly behind me. The road was empty. I began to walk a little faster, aware that I was being foolish. I had heard or seen nothing to make me believe there was anyone anywhere around. There was nothing on the northern tip of the island except Cliff House, and no one ever came that way unless it was for the purpose of visiting our family.

"You're paranoid," I told myself in disgust. "This business with Gordon and Natalie has gotten to you."

Still, I quickened my footsteps the way you do when someone is walking too close behind you, and I was almost running by the time I reached the path that led to the house.

I entered through the kitchen, which was just as it had been when I had left that morning, except that my mother had put the milk back in the refrigerator and my father had evidently fixed himself some eggs and bacon later in the day. Dad is a night person and Mother a day one, so their schedules don't coincide too well. Mother goes straight to her studio when we leave the house in the morning, and

Dad sleeps late and makes up for it by staying up and working half the night.

Now I could hear the sound of his typewriter rattling away behind the closed door of his office, and I knew better than to stop by and disturb him.

Instead, I climbed the stairs to the living room. Neal was there, sprawled on his stomach on the rug in the square patch of light from the west window, sketching.

"Hi," I said. "What are you working on?"

"I'm designing a castle." He was frowning, and his light brows were drawn together in concentration. When Neal draws, he is totally absorbed. In a moment, though, he lifted his head and looked up at me in surprise. "Did you just come in from outside?"

"Where else?" I said.

"How did you get there? I thought you were upstairs."

"How could I be upstairs when I'm just getting home from school?" I asked reasonably. "They don't give half-days to the high school students, you know."

"But Dad *said* you were upstairs. He said you didn't go to school today."

"Neal, really," I said, "you know perfectly well I went to school. I boarded the ferry when you did. No — actually, I was a little behind you — but we left the house together."

"That's what I told Dad, but he said you must have started feeling sick and come back."

"Where could he have gotten that idea?" I asked in bewilderment.

"He said he saw you."

"Now, wait a minute —" I began.

"No, honest, Laurie, he did. He said he spoke to you,

23

and you didn't answer. You just kept on going up the stairs to your room."

"To my room?" Here at last was something I could get a grip on. "There had better *not* be somebody in my room!" Leaving Neal staring after me, I hurried out of the living room and headed for the stairs.

CHAPTER 3

 THE DOOR TO MY ROOM WAS CLOSED, JUST as I had left it. I turned the knob, shoved it open, and stepped inside.

The room was awash with the golden light pouring in from the sliding glass doors leading out to the balcony. I glanced quickly about. Everything seemed just as it should be. I pushed the door softly closed behind me, and then suddenly the realization struck.

Someone had been here only moments before.

How I knew this, I could not have said. It was simply that her presence lingered like the echo of a voice or a perfume too subtle to be immediately recognized. She had stood, motionless, just as I did now, inspecting the room. My eyes tracked the route hers must have taken, moving from one of my possessions to another. The silly Mickey Mouse throw rug, left over from my early childhood. The environmental posters on the walls — the one of the redwood forest in California — the one of the fuzzy baby seal staring morosely out to sea. The orange and green throw pillows. The clutter on my bureau top. The jewelry box

Gordon had given me the month before for my birthday — his picture stuck in the border of the mirror — my hair dryer and brush, a pile of bobby pins, a bottle of nail polish.

My eyes moved farther, to the desk with my portable typewriter on it, to the shelves along the far wall, lined with books. She had crossed the room to stand in front of that shelf and read the titles. How did I know this? She had moved from there to the bed and seated herself on it and reached out her hand to run it over the surface of the pillow. The spread was smooth and taut. There was no indentation to show that someone had rested there.

But I knew. *I knew.*

Abruptly I flung open the door and went rushing out into the hall. There were footsteps on the stairs above me. I caught my breath, afraid to raise my eyes, and then I did raise them.

The familiar figure in jeans and a paint-spattered T-shirt was only my mother.

"Laurie, what's the matter?" she asked as she caught sight of my face.

"Someone's been in my room!" I announced, meeting her at the landing. "Someone's been in there going through my things!"

"Oh, hon, I don't think so," Mother said. "Neal doesn't do things like that, and Meg's over at the Burbanks'. She phoned after school to say she was going to be playing with Kimmie."

"I didn't mean to accuse the kids," I told her breathlessly. "It was somebody else — somebody who — who —" I let the sentence trail away, because I didn't know how to finish it. How could I say the words that had been in my mind: *It was somebody who looks like me?*

26

"Now, dear, you know there's been nobody here today but Dad and me," Mother said reasonably. "Mrs. DeWitt doesn't come to clean until Thursday. We can *ask* Neal —"

"It wasn't Neal." I followed her down the stairs to the living room and then down the second flight to the kitchen. "I'm sure it wasn't Neal."

"Oh, yuk," Mother said, glancing about at the remains of breakfast. "I didn't even rinse out the cereal bowls, did I? I just hate to waste that good morning light. There's going to be so little of it from now on with the days getting shorter." She plucked the bowls off the table and dumped them into the sink and turned on the hot water. "Your father might at least have cleared and rinsed things."

"Do I hear somebody using my name in vain?" Dad called from the office. At the end of the afternoon he worked with the door open so he could hear Mother when she came down from the studio. My parents work in separate areas of the house all day without ever seeing each other, and at the day's end they always have this big reunion.

"Hi, Jim," Mother called back, as pleased as though he had just gotten home from a long journey. "How did it go today?"

"Oh, not too bad," Dad said, emerging from the office hallway. "I managed to get the spaceship landed in Chapter Twelve. Alien invaders now slither through back alleys of Chicago, spreading diseases, the like of which you've never imagined. I stopped because I ran out of symptoms. I bet this one makes 'Movie of the Week.' "

"Dad," I said, "did you see somebody go into my room today?"

"Just you," Dad said.

"You couldn't have seen me. I wasn't here. I felt well

enough this morning to go to school, and I only got home about twenty minutes ago."

"Really? That's odd." He wrinkled his forehead the same way Neal does when he's perplexed. "Well, if you weren't here, I couldn't have seen you. You're right about that. It must have been yesterday."

"Neal said you told him —"

"I was mistaken, I guess. Had my mind on the new book. You know how I am sometimes." He went over to the refrigerator and opened the door and got out a bottle of white wine.

"While you're in there, could you get out the hamburger?" Mother asked. "What I was complaining about was your standing here this morning, watching your eggs cook, when you could have been rinsing dishes."

"I wasn't awake enough to think about that," Dad said.

He poured the wine into two glasses, and he and Mother sat down together at the kitchen table to hash over the events of the day, which was something that always bewildered me, because neither one of them had been anywhere or seen anybody. I left them there and went back up to the living room. Neal was still drawing. He had completed the front view of his castle and was working on a picture of it from another angle.

"I'm putting a dinosaur in the moat," he told me without looking up.

"That's a good idea."

I sat down in a chair by the picture window overlooking the sea. Directly below me the water frothed white around the base of the rocks. A gull came circling in, so close that its wing brushed against the glass, leaving a gray feather pinned there momentarily by the wind before a shift in air currents allowed it to slip away.

I was scared.

Someone had entered my life, and I didn't know who. The conclusion I had come to earlier that afternoon after talking with Jeff now had to be discarded. The fact that my father, too, had seen a girl like me — in a place I had not been — was too much to be coincidence. Cliff House was not kept locked during the day. It was possible that someone could have entered. The girl who had been on the beach the night before might have ascended the stairs, moving in and out of my father's sight as he stood, lost in his thoughts, planning the scene he was preparing to put on paper.

It could have happened. But — *why?*

If there was such a person — a Laurie Stratton look-alike — what was she doing here on Brighton Island now that the summer people were most of them gone? Why had she come here? When had she discovered her resemblance to me? What did she want from me and from the people whose lives were part of mine? Nothing had been removed from my room, of that I was certain. My possessions did not appear to have been tampered with. When I had looked about the room, everything had been in its accustomed place. It seemed almost as though this person had come visiting out of idle curiosity, to see where and how I lived.

Neal continued to draw. I sat in silence, struggling with questions that had no answers, while the sun sank lower and lower in the sky and the clouds began to soften and turn pink. After a while Meg came home. Her chirping voice came up the stairwell, describing the exciting first-day-in-third-grade events to the audience in the kitchen. Then Mother called Neal and me to the table, and we sat down to hamburgers and canned beans and what would have been a salad if Mother had gotten down to the grocery store in the village, but was instead lettuce with some chopped onion sprinkled over it.

"I lost track of time," she explained, not really apologetically. "One minute it was morning, and the next time I looked the day was almost over."

After dinner my parents and the kids played Monopoly at a card table in the living room. Any other evening I probably would have played with them, but tonight I was too upset to be able to concentrate. I needed to be alone to think, but I did not want to go to my bedroom.

Megan was in the process of purchasing Boardwalk when I went down the stairs and let myself out the kitchen door into the night.

Outside it was surprisingly light. The full moon that had lit up the beach for Gordon and Natalie the night before was at half-mast in the sky. After a moment or two of adjustment, I could see everything distinctly — the bushes, the sea oats, the sand path leading up from the road. The sound of the surf was very loud. I walked slowly along the side of the house to the point where the path stopped at the cliff's edge. There was no beach in front of Cliff House, just rocks, stair-stepping down tier by tier to the water. The highest of these were flat and dry and safe to stand on, but the lower ones were slimy with foam and seaweed. Once when he was very small Neal had slipped on one and taken a bad fall to the tier below. Between the rocks were crevices that led to hollows and caves where Megan liked to think mermaids lived. I knew better than to try to walk about, so

I just stood, quiet, listening to the waves breaking against the base of the cliff. The longer I stood there, the brighter the moonlight seemed to become. The white, swirling water had a luminescent quality that was hypnotic. If I gazed at it long enough, I thought, I might actually see a mermaid.

"Laurie?"

The voice spoke directly behind me, and I almost jumped out of my skin. Strong hands closed upon my shoulders. With a gasp of terror I tore myself free — and spun around to find myself facing Gordon.

"What's the matter?" he asked me.

"What do you *think* is the matter? You scared me to death!" My heart was pounding so hard I thought it might burst through the wall of my chest. "What are you doing here?"

"I wanted to talk to you," Gordon said.

"Then why didn't you phone?"

"I thought you might hang up on me, so I came over instead. I was just headed up the path to the house when I saw you standing out here on the rocks." He was staring hard at my face. "Say, look, something really is the matter, isn't it? You're not usually jumpy like this."

"No — really." I drew a long breath and let it out slowly. "It's just — well, it's been a messed-up day."

"It sure has," Gordon said. "Laurie, what I came over here to say was — well, I just want to tell you that it's okay."

"What's okay?"

"Whatever it was that you were doing last night. Not that I'm happy about it or anything. I'm jealous as hell. But it was true, what you said on the boat this afternoon. I don't

31

have any right to give you a hard time when I was out there with Nat."

"Are you in love with Nat?" I asked him.

"Of course not! She's a pretty girl — I'd had a few beers — my girlfriend had stood me up —"

"I didn't stand you up!" I objected.

"Let's not fight about it, Laurie. The point is, neither of us is lily white. We were both playing around a little. It wasn't anything for me — just a couple of kisses. What about you?"

"It wasn't even that for me," I said.

"Who was the guy?"

"I've told you and told you. There wasn't any guy."

"You want me to believe you were out there *alone*? That you'd break our date and miss the summer's best party just to go wandering the beach by yourself?"

"I don't care what you believe," I said wearily. "You're the one who said let's not fight. Did you come over here to make up or didn't you?"

"I don't know now. You're making it so tough." He put his hand under my chin and tilted my face up toward his. "Are you still my girl, Laurie?"

"I — I guess so," I said shakily. Jeff's words flashed through my mind — *He's got you on a string — he snaps his fingers and you jump.*

"That's what I wanted to hear." He lowered his head, and his mouth came down onto mine, and suddenly it didn't matter anymore whether he believed me or not, whether he had been with Natalie, whether he was pulling strings and snapping fingers — all that counted was that this was Gordon, my Gordon, and he was here now with his arms around me, and things between us were all right again.

We stayed for a long time out there in the moonlight. I didn't realize how long, until I went inside to be greeted by the sound of my father's typewriter rattling away on its evening stint. The living room, as I passed it, was dark and empty, the Monopoly game long over.

I paused at the door to the children's bedroom. The moonlight fell across Neal's pillow, painting his sleeping face with silver. His lips were parted, and he was breathing through his mouth with a whistling sound. In the bed across from him, Megan was lying crosswise, her feet thrust out from beneath the covers.

I went in and pulled her into a more comfortable position and drew the blanket over her. She came partly awake and reached up to touch my cheek.

"I saw you there — outside my window," she murmured sleepily.

"You did, did you?" I exclaimed, taken aback. "Don't you think that was pretty snoopy?"

Meg mumbled something indistinguishable and rolled over onto her stomach. Then abruptly she raised her head.

"You were up so high," she said clearly. "How did you get there?"

"I was — what?"

"High," she said, and sank back on her pillow and was immediately asleep.

I shook my head, bewildered as always by the directions eight-year-old minds can go, and more than a little irritated by the thought of my sister, standing at the window, absorbed in the sight of Gordon and me in the midst of our reconciliation scene. Tomorrow, I told myself, she and I are going to have a good, long talk.

I left the kids' room and continued up the stairs, passing

the open door to my parents' room, where Mother lay in bed, reading.

"'Night, hon," she called to me as I went by, and I called back, "Goodnight."

The next few steps brought me to the short hall leading to my own room. I moved along it gingerly and stopped in the doorway. The moonlight streamed through the east window to lie upon my bed, just as it had upon Neal's, and the rest of the room was sunk in shadows. I shivered slightly and reached around the door frame to switch on the overhead light.

Of course, there was no one there. Had I really thought there would be? Everything looked absolutely normal. The aura of the foreign presence I had sensed so strongly that afternoon seemed to have faded. I stepped into the room, feeling more comfortable than I had expected to, but I left the door standing open to afford contact with the rest of the house.

Suddenly I became aware of how terribly tired I was. The illness the night before and the long day filled with so much tension and confusion had left me drained and exhausted. I pulled off my clothes, let them lie where they fell, and got my pajamas out of the bureau. I put them on and picked up the brush from the bureau top, and then decided to bypass this nightly ritual.

Glancing across, I saw myself reflected in the sliding glass doors that led to the balcony. I stared at the reflection, wondering as I often did what it was that had won me Gordon. Why had he chosen me over Natalie and Darlene and Mary Beth and the others? The girl in the glass gazed back at me with wide, dark eyes. Her hand held a brush, half raised to her thick, black hair, and her body was slim and straight beneath the thin material of her summer pajamas. As I watched, the full mouth began to curve upward at the corners, as though this mirrored Laurie was pleased at what she saw.

It was not until I had turned off the light and climbed between the sheets that I realized what had been wrong with the picture.

The mouth on the reflected face had not been my mouth.

I had not been smiling.

CHAPTER 4

I SLEPT LITTLE THAT NIGHT. FOR A LONG time after I was in bed I lay trembling beneath the covers, trying to tell myself that the thing that I had seen could not have been so. Perhaps a warp in the glass, an angle of the light, a trick of my own eyes had altered the image. Perhaps I had smiled without realizing it. I had not been thinking about my expression as I stared at the reflection in the sliding door. I had been thinking about Gordon, about the fact that we were back together, that we had survived our first big misunderstanding without a break-up. I might have smiled at that thought, mightn't I? It would have been a natural thing to do.

Except that I knew I had not done it.

I thought of going down to the bedroom below mine and pouring the whole story out to Mother. Her company would be comforting, but what could she tell me except "You're imagining things, honey. A reflection is just that — a reflection. It does only what you do. You know that"? She would shrug off the situation the way she had that afternoon when I accosted her on the landing. "Oh, hon, I don't think so," she had said then, and tonight she would say it again, except sleepily, her mind already tuned down from the high energy level it reached in the mornings to the gentle, drowsy, relaxed plateau brought about by white wine and nightfall.

And what could I tell her that wouldn't sound ridiculous? What was it I wanted her to believe? That there was someone on the balcony, brushing her hair and smiling in at me? "So, let's go look," she would say sensibly, getting out of bed and reaching for her robe. "If there's somebody there, we certainly need to know about it." But there was no one there. I knew that already. From my bed I could see every inch of the balcony illuminated by moonlight, and it was empty.

When I did doze off at last, my sleep was fitful and filled with dreaming. They were strange dreams that seemed to overlap, running one into another and fitting together like pieces of a jigsaw puzzle, meaningless in themselves but building toward something that would be a whole. In one dream Gordon and I stood on a rock at the cliff's edge, and as I reached up for his kiss, I saw far above me Meg's face framed in her bedroom window. Her mouth kept opening and closing as though she were trying to shout a warning, but the roar of the surf was so loud that I could not hear. Then, suddenly, the rock beneath my feet tipped sharply. I grabbed for Gordon for support, but he stepped back away from me, and my hands closed upon empty air. Then I was falling, falling, for what seemed to be a million miles to the cold, churning water below.

Except, when I entered, it was not cold at all, but gentle and warm, and I did not have to struggle to keep afloat, for it held and rocked me. There was someone swimming beside me. At first I thought it was Gordon, but then I realized that it was someone much closer, someone who moved as I moved and stopped and rested when I rested. The rocking continued, and the water was gone, and it was my mother who was rocking me — but, no — it was not my mother — but a woman with long, dark hair hanging loose over her shoulders, and worried, deepset eyes.

"Can you see me?" asked a voice by my bed.

I opened my eyes. The moon had risen now above the level of my window, and the room was very dark.

"You do hear me, though, don't you?" the voice asked, and although I knew I had never heard it before, it was as familiar to me as my own.

"Are you the one with my face?" I whispered.

"I came first," she answered with a little laugh. "It's *you* who have *my* face."

"Who are you?" I asked her.

"You must know that. We are the two sides of a coin. We floated together in the same sea before birth. Didn't you know I would be coming for you one day?" There was a movement by my pillow. I felt the air stir against my face, and something as slight and soft as the breast feather of a gull brushed my forehead.

The next thing I knew, I was blinking at the ceiling, and the room was bright with sunlight.

The voice in my ears was Neal's.

"Mother says to get a move on, Laurie," he was saying from the doorway. "If you don't hurry up, you're going to miss breakfast."

This day was just as beautiful as its predecessor. I dressed and ate and went with the children to the ferry, and the breeze that struck my face as we left the shelter of the dunes should have been fresh enough to sweep the cobwebs away for anyone. But the dreams would not loose their hold on me. They lay upon me like a heavy blanket I could not shove off or wriggle my way out from under. When I saw Gordon waiting for me at the landing, there flashed through my mind not a vision of his face bent to mine in the moonlight, but a picture of him as he had been in my dream, jerking back from me as I grabbed for him to keep from falling. When I stood with him by the railing on the bow with his arm around my shoulders, it wasn't the blue water I saw stretching away to the mainland, but the thick, dark water that had held me afloat and rocked me.

"You're awfully quiet," Gordon said. "You're not still mad, are you? I thought we got everything straightened out."

"It's not that," I told him. "I didn't sleep very well last night, that's all. There have been some things happening around our place that have me sort of scared."

"You mean a prowler? Your folks had better start locking up in the daytime. As wrapped up as they get in the stuff they do, somebody could walk right in there and rip them off, and they'd never know a thing about it."

He was repeating something he'd heard said in the village, I was sure. There were many people who thought the Stratton family pretty strange. How could two people live as my parents did, shut away in an extravagant house on the tip of the island, with apparently no interest in anything except each other and their children and their work? Dad and Mother had never joined the Yacht Club, which was where most people went to socialize. Although they could easily have afforded one, they had never bothered to buy a boat, even a little outboard. They had permitted me to take out a junior membership at the Tennis Club, because all my friends played there, but they themselves never showed up to watch the meets. They didn't go to Brighton Inn for dinner or dancing, and if they went to the beach, nobody knew it.

"My folks aren't exactly stupid," I said, trying to treat the subject lightly. "They'd know if people were tramping in and out of the house carting out the furniture."

"Don't make a joke of it, Laurie," Gordon said. "I'm serious. Your mom's up in her studio, and your dad's shut off with his typewriter all day, and they're *out* of it. People probably *could* haul off the furniture without their knowing. And if you're in the habit of wandering around by yourself at night, that's not good sense. All kinds of things could happen. You and I were outside for hours last night, and your folks never even stuck their heads out to check on you."

"They trust me," I said.

"That has nothing to do with it. What if you hadn't been with me? What if some creep had sneaked up on you there on the rocks? Jeff Rankin, for instance?"

"That's ridiculous," I said irritably. "Jeff would never hurt anybody."

"You can't know that. He's turned real weird since the accident; everybody says so. And if not him, then somebody else, some stranger. You're so alone out there, you could scream your head off and there'd be nobody to hear you." He tightened his arm around me. "I care about you, Laurie. I don't want something to happen to you."

"I know that." The things he'd been saying were true, of

course. We did need to start being more careful. But the girl — I had begun thinking of her as "the mirror girl" — would not be stopped by a lock on the door, of that I was certain. It was the *only* thing I was certain about.

I wished I could talk to Gordon, really talk to him, but I knew that was impossible. He'd think I was crazy, and maybe he would be right. Wasn't that what crazy people did, imagine things that couldn't be real? But if I followed that line of reasoning, then Gordon himself must be crazy, and Natalie, and my father. And Megan. What was it she had said? "You were up so high"? I had thought that was sleep talk, but now I wondered. Who was it she had seen last night, me or the mirror girl? What had she meant by my being "up high"? Gordon and I had been standing below her window.

"Where's my sister?" I said, pulling back from the railing. "I need to ask her something."

"What's the matter with you?" Gordon said, stiffening. "Can't you stand here and talk to me without getting jumpy? You don't need to chase down Meg. You were with her at breakfast. It's somebody else you want to go looking for, isn't it?"

"Somebody else?" I repeated blankly.

"That guy you were on the beach with. It is, isn't it? Is he one of the island guys? Look, Laurie, you play straight with me. I told you about Nat —"

"Oh, Gordon, go to hell!"

There was a moment's silence. I could not believe I'd said such a thing.

Then Gordon asked quietly, "Do you mean that?"

"No — no, I don't. I'm sorry." Here we were, back together again, and already I was wrecking things. What did I want to do anyway, hand Gordon over to Natalie on a silver platter? He was suspicious of me, and why shouldn't he be? He'd seen me with his own eyes at a place I kept denying I had been.

"I'm really sorry," I said again. "Like I said, I didn't get much sleep last night, and I'm tired and edgy, and you keep accusing me of things that aren't so."

"Okay, okay," Gordon said placatingly. "Do you want me to go find Meg for you?"

"No," I told him. "I'll talk to her later at the landing."

But when the ferry docked there was such a hectic mass exodus that no one could have found anybody, and by the time I did see Meg, she was encircled by her cronies, all squealing and banging lunch pails and trotting off in a herd toward the elementary school.

The day had started badly; it continued to get worse. I forgot my locker combination and had to attend my first two classes without books, which did little to endear me to my teachers. I did manage to catch Helen in the hall after second period, and she worked the lock, so I entered third period with algebra book in hand, but my mind was in such turmoil that I missed every problem that was given me. In fourth period, English, I realized I had left that morning without lunch money.

"Don't worry about it," Helen said as I shuffled through the contents of my purse. "I've got enough for both of us. You can pay me back tomorrow."

So when the bell rang we went to the cafeteria together, which meant that when we came through the line I had the choice of sitting alone with Helen as I had the day before or taking her with me to the table where the island kids were gathered. Either one was going to make problems. There was an unspoken understanding that the students from the mainland sat at that table only by special invitation, which was pretty much decided upon by the group as a whole. At the same time, now that Gordon and I had patched things up, it would seem strange for me to turn my back on the group he went around with and go sit in the corner with some girl I hardly knew.

"Let's take our trays over there," I said to Helen, nodding toward the table.

She followed my gaze, surprised. "I thought you said that was a clique."

"It is," I told her. "But I'm sort of a part of it. At least, Gordon, the guy I go with, is."

"Which one is he?" Helen asked. "Not *him?*" as Blane Savage glanced up from his overloaded plate and zeroed in on us as we stood there, balancing our trays.

"No, Gordon doesn't eat this period. He's got B lunch," I said. "But these kids are nice too. Come on, let's go over. It'll give you a chance to meet some people."

It was a bad decision. I knew that the moment we reached the table.

"Hi, everybody," I said, setting down my tray in the space across from Darlene. "This is my lockermate, Helen Tuttle. She's new this year. These are Darlene — Blane — Mary Beth —" I continued to make introductions the length of the table.

Blane mumbled something that passed for a greeting and bit into his sandwich.

Darlene said, "Hello," in that sweet, soft voice of hers that always sounded as though she were a little surprised. I watched her eyes go up to the top of Helen's head, which was about four inches higher than mine, and work their way down over the rust-colored hair, the light blue eyes with their almost invisible brows and lashes, the pleasant, freckled face, the neck encircled by a silver chain from which there hung a little turquoise carving. Then they took the long plunge to the large feet, encased in socks and saddle shoes. She and Mary Beth exchanged amused glances.

"Hello," Helen said unselfconsciously and began unloading her tray.

"Helen's from the Southwest," I said as I took my seat, hoping I didn't sound apologetic. "She's just beginning to learn what it's like to be a New Englander."

Mary Beth looked amused. "You don't become a New Englander simply by moving here." She paused and then added without much interest, "Where in the Southwest are you from, Helen?"

"Tuba City," Helen told her. "That's in Arizona on the Navajo reservation. My parents taught at the Indian boarding school."

"My goodness!" Darlene exclaimed politely. "That must have been interesting." Then she turned to Blane and started talking about the weekend sailing meet, and Mary Beth directed her attention to the other end of the table, and that was that for Helen.

· Not that it seemed to bother her. She just kept on eating and didn't appear to notice that she was being excluded from the conversation. She kept her ears open, though, and on the way back to class she said, "It must be fantastic living on an island."

"It is," I told her. "It's really beautiful out there. You'll have to take the ferry over sometime before the weather changes and it's too cold to enjoy the beaches."

"That would be great," Helen said. "When would you like me to come?"

That was when I realized that Mary Beth had been right about New Englanders; you didn't become one just by moving across the country. Nobody I knew would have taken my casual comment as an invitation for a personal visit.

"Oh, I don't know," I said awkwardly. "Not this weekend. I'm going to be crewing for Gordon during the sailing race."

"Any time that's good for you will be fine for me," Helen assured me. "I don't know enough people yet to have made plans to do anything."

"Let's just leave it open for now," I said, "and I'll let you know."

Even as I spoke, I knew that I wouldn't be able to get out of it. I was going to end up having Helen as a houseguest. And as good-natured and likable as she appeared to be, I didn't want her. There was no way in the world she was going to fit in with the crowd from the island, and I had serious doubts about how she would go over with my parents. They were so protective of their privacy and their work schedules, entertaining an outsider would not be their idea of pleasure.

So the day dragged by with one stupid irritation piling upon another. Little things, but provoking. The heel came loose on my shoe, and a bra strap broke. A felt pen came open in my purse and leaked all over everything. On the ferry ride back to the island, Natalie plunked herself down on the seat on the far side of Gordon to finish an "interesting conversation" they had started over lunch, and I suddenly realized that they shared the same lunch period and would

probably be eating together every day. It didn't exactly make me jealous. After all, they were friends, weren't they? Why shouldn't they eat together? Still, the thought of it made me uncomfortable, especially when I recalled those "few kisses" they had exchanged the night of Nat's party and the fact that Gordon hadn't seemed to feel all that guilty about them.

We split forces at the landing area, with Gordon and Nat and the rest of them all headed toward the village, and Meg, Neal, and me headed out to Cliff House. Neal took off immediately on those winged feet of his, and I had Meg to myself.

"I want to ask you something," I said to her. "Last night when I was pulling up your blanket, you said something about my being up 'high.' What did you mean by that?"

"I don't remember you pulling up my blanket," Meg said.

"That part doesn't matter," I told her. "You were half asleep. The thing is, I did go into your room, and you did talk about my being 'high up.' You must have meant something." I paused and then prodded gently. "You said you looked out the window. You were peeking at Gordon and me, right?"

"I was not!" Meg exclaimed hotly. "I didn't even know Gordon was over. He never came in the house." She was so outraged at my accusation that I almost believed her.

"He *was* over, though," I said, trying to sound casual. "So if you looked out the window you must have seen us together."

"I didn't look out the window," Megan said. "*You* looked *in*."

"In your window? That's impossible. I would have had to have been standing on a ladder."

"That's what I couldn't understand," Meg said. "You were up so high. How did you get there?"

The crazy thing was, her response did not surprise me. I had actually been expecting it. I was becoming numb to surprises. I felt the way you do when you are moving through a dream and the most impossible things are happening and you are accepting them as normal. Perhaps I *was* dreaming. Perhaps if I hung on long enough and kept myself calm and tried not to be too frightened, my eyes would snap open and I would find myself back where I had been two days ago on the morning after stomach flu with school about to start and everything in my life in order.

But, of course, that did not happen.

As I was drifting off to sleep that night, I became conscious of the girl's presence at my bedside. I could not see her in the darkness, but I knew that she was there.

"Who are you?" I asked her. "What is your name? What shall I call you?"

I felt her lean across me, and her breath was light against my cheek.

"I am Lia," she whispered. "I am your sister."

CHAPTER 5

 AND THEN FOR MANY NIGHTS SHE DID NOT come again, my sister Lia.

My sister Lia?

I had a small, plump sister named Megan Stratton, a light-haired little girl with sky blue eyes and a sprinkling of freckles across her nose. I had been there to welcome her when my parents brought her home from the hospital, tiny and red-faced, howling lustily from the depths of a fuzzy blue receiving blanket that had at one time been Neal's. I had no dark, strange Lia for a sister. Even in dreams I could not, would not, accept her. She was no part of me.

"Go away!" I told her fiercely as she leaned across my bed. "Go somewhere else, whoever you are. I will not have you here!"

And — she was gone.

There was no movement, no rustle of sound to signify her leaving. It was simply that one moment she was there beside me in the darkness, and the next, she was not.

I drew a long breath and let it slowly out again in a silent •

sigh, and turned my face into my pillow. I slept that night without dreaming. And the next night, and the next as well. By the end of the week I was able to tell myself that it was over. I was rid of the crazy obsession that had gripped me. The mirror girl had left me. I was free.

That weekend I crewed for Gordon at the sailing races. We came in third, because we had some problems maneuvering the final buoy. The following week I invited Helen to come out the next Saturday to tour the island and stay overnight at Cliff House. Since the visit was inevitable, I could see nothing to be gained by postponing it. Besides, as the days passed, Helen and I were getting to be better and better friends.

To my surprise, my parents didn't seem at all disturbed by the prospect of a houseguest.

"We can set up a cot for her in your room," Dad said. "Just be sure she understands the way we live and doesn't expect to be entertained."

"I've explained things to her," I assured him. "Helen's so easygoing, anything's okay with her."

"It's nice you have a new friend," Mother said, and she even made some vague reference to baking a cake "if I can get around to it." I knew it wouldn't happen, but the thought was hospitable.

It was Gordon who objected to the visit.

"You don't mean you're going to be stuck with her overnight?" he demanded irritably. "I thought we'd talked about taking in a movie on the mainland Saturday."

"We can still do that," I said. "Why don't you try to fix Helen up with a date?"

"Somebody six-foot-ten with failing eyesight?"

49

"That's mean," I said. "She's no beauty queen, but she's really nice. Rennie isn't dating anybody special, is he?"

"Rennie wouldn't be seen dead with Helen Tuttle," Gordon told me. "He likes his chicks cute and cuddly. What have you latched onto that loser for, anyway, Laurie? Even the girls don't like her. Mary Beth says she's pushy as hell."

"She isn't pushy," I corrected him. "She's just friendly. People are a lot more outgoing where she's from. What about Tommy? He's tall, and that summer girl he was going with went back to Vermont."

"Forget it," Gordon said. "It's not worth the effort. I don't want to spend Saturday night dragging Helen around. Have a great weekend with your good buddy, and I'll see you Monday."

The conversation left me feeling depressed and sort of empty inside, but the sight of Helen's face when she arrived on the Saturday morning ferry was enough to lift my spirits considerably. Her red hair was wild from the wind, and her eyes were shining.

"That was really something!" she exclaimed, clambering onto the dock and almost dropping her canvas overnight bag into the water. "Captain Ziegler — isn't he Mary Beth's father? — was great. He let me sit with him in the cabin and do part of the steering. And the rest of the time I rode up top where I could see all over! Do you know this is the first time in my life I've been on a boat?"

"You're kidding!" I said incredulously.

"No, it's true. The only water we had back home ran down the arroyos after a rainstorm. I can't get used to the idea that you take a ferry to school the way I used to take a bus." She drew in a deep breath of the sea air. "It smells so clean. You're so lucky, Laurie, actually living year-round in this beautiful place!"

When she caught her first glimpse of Cliff House from the bend in the road, she was even more ecstatic. "It looks like a castle out of a fairy tale!" she exclaimed. The closer we got, the more enthusiastic she became. With each step up the curving stairway, she was gasping and exclaiming, and when we entered the living room, she gave a spontaneous cry of delight.

"It's simply beautiful!"

In the years since we had moved to the island, I had come to take our home more or less for granted. Now, however, I found myself seeing it as though for the first time, through the eyes of a newcomer — the high, weathered beams running the width of the ceiling; the marvelous stone fireplace flanked by two of Mother's haunting seascapes; the expanse of picture window facing out upon the sea.

"Mother's upstairs working," I said to explain the lack of inhabitants. "My brother, Neal, is too; he takes painting lessons from her on Saturday mornings. Dad sleeps in because he writes nights, and my sister —"

"Is right here!" Megan announced loudly, popping up from the far side of the sofa. "I've been teaching school, and it's snack-time. My students are starving."

I introduced her to Helen, and the three of us went down to the kitchen, where Meg went through the ritual of juice-and-crackering herself and a menagerie of stuffed animals, while Helen and I made peanut butter and jelly sandwiches and loaded them into a backpack.

Dad came downstairs before we were finished, greeted Helen pleasantly if sleepily, and got his eggs out of the refrigerator.

"Are you girls off on a picnic?" he asked.

"I thought we'd take the bikes the length of the island," I told him.

"Fine — fine. Sounds like a good plan. I'll see the two of you at dinner, then." His mind was already slipping away to focus on his world of aliens.

I slid my arms through the straps of the pack, hoisted it to my shoulders, and led Helen down to the storage shed where the kids and I kept our bicycles. I let her have my ten-speed and took Neal's smaller bike for myself, and we set off.

We covered the island that day, from Cliff House at the northern point to the vacated summer cottages at the southern end. The sun burned down on our heads, and I could practically see new freckles popping out on Helen's face and arms as we pedaled along. We stopped several times to pick wild grapes and some last remaining blueberries, and for Helen to examine fishnets drying in the sun. We ate our lunch in a hollow between the dunes on the east side of the island, and, leaving our shoes with the bikes, walked along the beach at the water's edge where the icy surf lapped up to attack our toes.

Later we lay sprawled in the sand and talked, and I began to discover what it was like to have a nonjudgmental friend to confide in, someone to whom I was myself, not "Gordon Ahearn's girlfriend."

We talked about school — our families — and, of course, boys. I told Helen how shy and unattractive I had felt when I was younger, and how much my life had changed when Gordon started dating me.

Helen told me about a boy named Luis Nez.

"That was the name he used at school," she said. "I

wasn't allowed to know his Indian name. The Navajos are a private people. Luis was my boyfriend, but there was so much he couldn't share with me." She paused, and then raised her hand to touch the tiny turquoise carving at her throat. "When I left, he gave me this."

"What is it?" I asked, hoisting myself up on one elbow so as to see better.

"A fetish," Helen said. "It's an eagle, predator of the air. When Luis learned we were coming east by plane, he carved it for me. Turquoise is the Navajo good-luck stone. A turquoise eagle protects the wearer against evil spirits from the skies."

"It must have been hard for you to move away," I said.

"It was, of course. But I know it was for the best. I was getting to care too much, and it could never have worked. It was fun living on the reservation when I was little. The differences didn't matter so much then. Later — well, do you remember that first day we ate lunch together, and I said to you that there are cliques everywhere?"

"I remember," I said.

"It's even worse when it's a culture thing. You can't break through."

"You didn't have girlfriends?"

"Not ones I could talk to."

"I've never had friends like that either," I said, realizing it fully for the first time. Darlene and Mary Beth and Natalie were surface friends. They had permitted me to become part of their world because of Gordon, but if and when Gordon decided he was tired of me, I would be out of it again.

"Nat's had her claws out for Gordon since before I started going with him," I told Helen. "Just a few weeks ago she gave a party. I was sick and couldn't go, and the minute my back was turned —" And there I was, spilling out the whole story — Nat and Gordon on the beach — the "few kisses" Gordon had confessed to — and then, because it followed naturally and was so much a part of my thoughts these days, I told her about the girl they had thought was I.

"But it wasn't," I said. "I was home in bed the whole time."

"You weren't using astral projection, were you?" Helen asked.

"Using what?" I said in bewilderment.

"You know — sending your mind out from your body? Luis's father used to be able to do it." She paused. "If you had, you'd have known it. It's something you have to work at."

"I don't know what you're talking about," I said. "What did Luis's father *do?*"

"I'm not sure exactly," Helen said. "Luis didn't talk much about it. He seemed to take it for granted. The medicine men could do it whenever they wanted, I think, and some of the others too. The way Luis described it, the person has to *will* himself out of his body. It takes tremendous concentration."

"I still don't understand," I said.

"Well, think of it this way. It's like the soul leaving the body when you die. It lifts and goes, right? Except that with astral projection you're not dead. The soul or mind or whatever you want to call it — the *identity* part of you — is focused away, just for a short while, and then comes back."

"Where does it go?"

"Wherever you want to be. Distance doesn't make any difference. Luis told me that when his little brother was

54

born, their father was away on a hunting trip. The baby wasn't expected for another month. When his mother was in labor, she looked up and saw her husband standing at the end of the bed, smiling down at her."

"That's wishful thinking," I said. "She must have wanted him there so much she dreamed him up. There's nothing so unusual about that."

"It wasn't like that," Helen insisted. "When Luis's father came home two days later, he knew all about the baby — exactly when it had been born and that it was a boy — *everything. He had been there!*"

"He couldn't have been," I said. "There has to be some other explanation."

"I know it's hard to accept, but a lot of Christian beliefs are too, if you haven't been raised with them. The Virgin birth, for instance, and water turning into wine. I told my parents what Luis said. Dad's the one who gave me that term, 'astral projection.' Luis didn't call it that. Dad says there are people doing scientific studies on it, so it can't be all that far out."

"Maybe not," I conceded. "Still, it has nothing to do with me. I wasn't 'projecting' anywhere that night. I was crashed out."

"Okay, I believe you," Helen said. "Do you think we should start back pretty soon now? I'd really like to see the village."

"It's right on the way," I told her. "Most of the tourist shops are still open, and there's even an art gallery. Mother has some of her work there — the paintings she hasn't sent to New York."

We got to our feet, brushing off the sand as well as we could, and wheeled the bikes back to the Beach Road.

Helen was right; it was later than I had thought it was. I had lost track of time, and the sun had been sliding steadily down the sky as we had lain talking.

On the outskirts of the village we passed the Rankin cottage. Jeff was out in the front yard, slapping blue paint on the shutters. He had a visored cap pulled down over his forehead to protect his face from the sun.

I waved casually, and Helen called, "Hi!"

Jeff turned, surprised, and raised the paintbrush in greeting.

"What are *you* doing here?"

"Visiting Laurie," Helen called back. "I came over on the ferry."

"Glad you told me that. I thought you swam!"

"You nut!" Helen said, laughing.

"How do you know him?" I asked her as we pedaled on. "I've never seen him act so friendly."

"He sits in front of me in second period. Rankin — Tuttle — you know, alphabetically. We kid around. Is that place over there a hotel?"

"It's the Brighton Inn," I said. "Natalie's dad owns it. You've got to see the inside. The ocean water runs right through like a creek, and they've got a little bridge built over. That building across the street is the gallery. The painting in the window is one of Mother's."

By the time I had finished giving Helen a guided tour of the village it was really late, and we headed back to Cliff House, pedaling as fast as we could to beat the descending dark. We put the bikes away and entered the house through the kitchen. Dad was seated at the table, getting ready to pour wine, and Mother was burning a chicken under the broiler. Both of them were in good spirits — their work had gone well — and Mother had a painting of Neal's to show us. It was a strange, fantasy thing of rocks that were shaped like dragons.

"It's good, isn't it?" she said with satisfaction.

"He's our kid, all right," Dad acknowledged, "half artist, half sf nut."

"Sf?" Helen asked, mystified.

"That's short for science fiction," Mother told her. "The other term is 'sci-fi,' but don't use that unless you want a fight on your hands. It's a put-down unless it's used by another writer."

Dad came back at her with some reference to artists, and the kids heard us laughing and came rushing down the stairs to see what they were missing. Dad brought out two more wineglasses for Helen and me — "After all, it's not every night we have company for dinner" — and Mother flipped the chicken to blacken it on the other side, and everything settled into a regular family-type evening.

My parents liked Helen. I could tell by the way they joked around with her.

"So you're from Arizona, are you?" Dad said. "The state of tumbleweeds and dust storms. We took a trip out that way once and dried out and wrinkled up like a couple of prunes."

"Speak for yourself, Jim," Mother said. "I really liked it. We almost settled there, remember? If we had, I'd be painting mesas and mountains instead of ocean."

"You almost settled in Arizona?" I asked in surprise. "You never told me that."

"It wasn't Arizona," Mother said. "It was New Mexico. It was back before you came along, in Dad's and my starvation days. We got this idea that we might build a

57

hogan or something and live there on beans and chiles while we were waiting for the world to appreciate us."

"You had starvation days?" Helen asked incredulously. I guess she thought Cliff House had always been ours.

"All creative people do their share of starving," Dad said. "When Shelly and I were first married we lived in a studio walk-up in Greenwich Village and survived on peanut butter. That's how my wife came to be the cook she is today. By the time she hit the big time and could afford to feed me something better, it was too late for her to learn how to manage an oven."

"When *I* hit the big time!" Mother exclaimed, tossing a chicken bone across the table at him in mock anger. "It was when *Walk to the Stars* sold to television that things changed for us. They got Kerry Arquette for the lead role —"

"Just about the same time your work was getting recognized." Dad grinned, frankly delighted for both of them. "It all seemed to come at once, Helen, like catsup out of a bottle. You shake and shake, and it seems like nothing's ever going to happen, and then — blurp! — it's all there. Money started coming in, and we knew right away what we wanted to do with it. We had a dream. To live on an island. To be together, away from disturbances — to work — to raise our kids."

" 'Kid' then," Mother reminded him.

"Right. Laurie then, and we thought there'd never be another. And then, out of the blue, blown in from Saturn —"

"Oh, Dad, cool it," Neal said, blushing. He never liked to be the subject of a conversation.

Dad reached over and ruffled his fine blond hair.

"It was a good wind that blew us you and Megan," he told him fondly.

After dinner we sat in the living room and played poker, which was one of my mother's favorite card games. I was never able to understand why, because she played so badly. Helen proved to be even worse, her animated face giving away every draw, so all you had to do was look at her to know exactly what was in her hand. The children found this so hilarious they were overcome by giggles, and Neal finally ended up falling out of his chair with his pile of poker chips flying in all directions.

"It's not always this wild around here," I told Helen as we were preparing for bed.

"Oh, I enjoyed it," she assured me. "I'm an only child, and things can get pretty dull around our place. You're lucky to have a brother and sister." She paused and then added thoughtfully, "They don't resemble you at all, do they? They're both of them so fair."

"Like Dad and Mother," I said. "Heredity's a funny thing, isn't it?"

Dad had set up the cot and put an air mattress on it and a pile of blankets. Even so, it didn't look all that comfortable, so I decided to take it myself and give Helen the bed. She argued a little but gave in without too much pressure; we were both of us so tired after our long day's cycling that we were prepared to settle anywhere.

Once in bed with the light off, we exchanged a few mumbled sentences. Helen commented about the roar of the surf — "It sounds like it's coming right in through the front door" — and I laughed and told her, "I'm so used to it, I never hear it." Once I'd said that, though, I *did* begin to hear it — the rush and the crash and the soft sucking sound as the waves moved in and out against the rocks.

Somewhere once I had read a description of Eternity —

"If there were a mile-high mountain of granite, and once every ten thousand years a bird flew past and brushed it with a feather, by the time that mountain was worn away, a fraction of a second would have passed in the context of Eternity."

That had stuck in my mind, and it came back to me now as I listened drowsily to the waves dragging upon the great black rocks at the base of Cliff House. How many eons would pass before those rocks were gone? Cliff House itself along with the people who had lived there would by then be long forgotten. The whole of Brighton Island would probably have been swept away by winds and tides. Would there still be a mainland with people upon it — and, if so, what sort of people? Humans like us, or a whole new civilization straight out of the pages of one of Dad's novels? "A fraction of a second . . . in the context of Eternity . . ."

My mind rocked slowly back and forth at the edge of sleep, and I was just beginning to slip over and sink beneath the waves when Helen spoke my name.

"Laurie," she said, "what are you doing there?"

My eyes flew open and I blinked hard into the darkness. "What?"

"Please, get back! Don't look at me that way? What *is* it?"

"Helen," I said, "wake up! You're having a dream."

I reached over and groped for the bedside lamp and then realized that I was on the cot on the far side of the room, so I got up and went to the door and flicked on the overhead.

Helen was sitting bolt upright in bed. She raised her arm automatically to shield her eyes from the influx of light, and then lowered it again as she focused upon me.

"You're over there," she said.

"I had to get up to reach the light switch."

"You were on the cot?"

"Of course. Where did you think I was?" I crossed over to the bed and sat down on the side of it and reached for her hand. It was trembling. "You were having a nightmare."

"No, I wasn't," Helen said. "I was wide awake. I had dozed off, and then I felt something brush against my cheek. I opened my eyes, and you were here, standing next to the bed. You were looking down at me, and you had the strangest expression — not like yourself at all."

"I never moved from the cot," I said. "Not until you called my name."

"But I saw you!"

"How could you?" I asked, trying to be reasonable. I fought to keep my voice steady. "There's no moon tonight. It was totally dark."

"But there was a light — some sort — there had to have been. It was like — like it was coming from inside — but, that's impossible, isn't it?" Helen's hand gripped mine tightly. "It wasn't you, Laurie. I know that now. There was a girl here, and she looked like you. On the surface she did. She had your features, your hair — but her eyes —" She broke off the sentence and started to shake her head frantically from side to side. Her red hair flew back and forth like a Raggedy Ann wig. "It wasn't you — it was somebody else."

"A nightmare," I said again tentatively, but we both

knew that was not true. The mirror girl had been there, and Helen had seen her, not as a shadow, a formless voice in the darkness, but in my shape and form.

"Her eyes?" I whispered. "What *about* her eyes?"

"That's what frightened me," Helen said in a choking voice. "I wouldn't have been scared to wake in your home and find you by the bed, for heaven's sake. That would have been natural enough. People get up in the night, bumble around, try to find the bathroom, come back half asleep to the bed they're used to. What scared me were the eyes. They were evil eyes, Laurie, stark evil! When she stood looking down at me, all I could think was — *this person is going to kill me!*"

CHAPTER 6

WE TALKED ABOUT IT DURING THE WEEKS that followed, first in that shaky, self-conscious way people do when they are afraid of a subject, and later, when we had had a chance to draw away from it a bit, more objectively. Who could the girl have been? How could she have gotten into the room and left it so quickly? What did it all mean?

Of course, by then I had told Helen the entire story, not just the part about Gordon and Natalie.

"I've been scared I might be going crazy," I said, admitting that to myself for the first time. "The dreams — and that's what I kept telling myself they were — were taking over my life."

"You're not crazy," Helen said firmly. "And that girl you call Lia isn't any dream. Have you ever actually seen her?"

"No, not really. As a shadow, maybe. As a reflection. Not as a real person."

"I saw her clearly," Helen said. "Either I'm more attuned to such things than you are, or else she's getting stronger. If that's the case, she'll soon be able to appear anywhere, even in broad daylight."

"What do you mean?" I asked nervously. "You can't be talking about — about that 'astral projection' thing. I told you, I can't do that."

"But Lia can," Helen said. "There *is* a Lia, Laurie. She's not just somebody your mind has invented. If she were, I wouldn't have seen her too. Somewhere in the world she exists, this girl who looks so exactly like you, and she has learned how to project herself."

"There can't be somebody who looks that much like me," I objected.

"An identical twin would."

"That's ridiculous," I said. "I don't have any twin."

Helen regarded me thoughtfully. "Are you certain?"

"That's the silliest thing I've ever heard," I said vehemently. "Of course I'm certain."

"Do you have a better suggestion?"

"No, but anything, just anything, would make more sense than that."

I would have given a lot to have been able to discuss the subject with Gordon, but the one time I tried to broach it, he closed me off quickly.

"When Helen spent the night with me —" I began.

"I don't want to talk about Helen," Gordon interrupted. "You're so wrapped up in that weirdo, it's starting to look funny to everybody. Mary Beth says you don't even eat at the table with the island bunch anymore. You go off and sit with Helen in a corner."

"Why should that bother you?" I asked him.

"I just told you why — because it looks funny. You've

got nice friends, and you act like you don't want to be with them. It's insulting."

"They're your friends," I said.

"If they're mine, they're yours. At least, they've tried to be." He regarded me worriedly. "What's happened to you, Laurie? You're just not the way you used to be. When we're together I don't feel like you're really with me. It's like your mind's off somewhere else."

"I'm with you now," I said, and kissed him to prove it.

That always worked with Gordon. His mouth came down so hard on mine that I could feel my teeth cutting into my upper lip. I guess it was what you would call a passionate kiss, but in the middle of it I realized that he was right — my mind was detaching itself — moving away from the two of us as though it had business elsewhere. Somehow I seemed to be standing back, looking at this boy and girl kissing, thinking what a good-looking couple they made, like something out of a movie, perfectly cast, with the boy's fair head so nicely contrasting with the girl's dark one.

This is how Lia must feel, I found myself thinking. She stands apart and watches.

The thought was so terrifying that I shivered convulsively, and Gordon broke off the kiss to draw back and stare at me.

"I must really turn you on! I kiss you, and you shudder. That's really great for the old ego, I can tell you."

"I'm sorry," I said. "You know it wasn't that."

"Then what the hell *was* it? That's what I meant — your mind's never *here* anymore. I don't know what your problem is, Laurie, but if you can't get it together soon, we're going to have to call it quits. Things can't go on the way they are."

"No," I agreed, "they can't."

It was not only my relationship with Gordon that I was referring to. As important as that had been to me, it was overshadowed now by other issues. Helen's suggestion had been absurd, but I would have to confront it in order to discard it. As she herself had said, I had no alternatives to offer. My parents might laugh at me, or be hurt and angry, or get worried and haul me over to the mainland to see a psychiatrist, any of which was better than being left to finger over and over again the strange little lump of doubt that had been planted at the corner of my mind. If there was really a Lia, and if she was, indeed, my sister, I had to know.

The next afternoon when I got home from school, I went up the stairs to Mother's studio.

I entered without knocking, which is what she prefers ("Banging on the door is the last thing you want to do when somebody has a brushful of paint in her hand," she always says). The room was filled with the slanted, golden light which is so much mellower than the blue-white light of morning. Mother was seated at her easel with her back to me. On the canvas before her there was the first rough outline of beach and ocean and the figure of a child. I could tell by the lines of the sturdy body that it was Megan, bent forward, hands on knees, gazing intently at something that had been washed up by the tide. The sky was gray and foreboding, as though a storm were rising in the distance. Mother always painted her skies first and then worked her way into the foreground of her pictures.

I drew a long breath and let her have the question.

"Do I have a twin?"

For a long moment Mother gave no sign of having heard me. She continued to sit motionless, the hand that was holding the brush frozen in midair a scant half-inch from the surface of the canvas. Then, slowly, she turned to face me.

"Why do you ask such a thing?"

"Because I need to know."

"You don't come up with a question like that out of the blue. Something or somebody had to lead you to ask it."

"Does that really matter?" The fact that she had not given an immediate denial was answer enough. I stared at her, incredulous. "What happened to her? Where is she? How could you never have told me?"

"There didn't seem to be any reason why you should know," Mother said. Her face was very pale, and her eyes had the wide, startled look that Neal's get when he is confronted with something that he does not know how to handle. "The whole thing is so long behind us, and we had no choice. We couldn't take both of you. We couldn't even afford one baby, really, but we wanted you so desperately —"

"You couldn't *take* us!" I repeated. "Take us *where?*" A second possibility occurred to me, and I heard my voice rising in an unnatural squeak that sounded like someone in a soap opera. "*Am I adopted?*"

"Oh, Lord, I've really messed things up now, haven't I?" Mother shook her head miserably. "When you came in here asking about a twin, I thought that, of course, if you'd discovered that, then you knew the circumstances. I'd never have broken it to you like this. Let's go get Dad. We'll all three of us sit down together and talk it through, and he'll explain —"

"I *am* adopted, aren't I? Tell me!"

"Yes." Mother started to get to her feet, her arms reaching out for me, but I motioned her back.

"You've lied to me! For seventeen years, you've lied!"

"That's not so," Mother said. "We never lied, we simply didn't tell you. Why should we? You're our child just as much as your brother and sister. We couldn't love you more if I'd carried you in my body. There never seemed to be any reason to set you to wondering and worrying over things that should have no bearing on your life." She paused and then added pleadingly, "Let's go downstairs now, Laurie. Your father can explain it all better than I can."

"You mean the man I've always *thought* of as 'my father,' " I said cruelly, wanting to hurt her, to repay her for the terrible hurt she had just inflicted upon me. "He's Neal's and Megan's father, not mine."

"He's your father in every way that counts," Mother said.

And so we went down, and she got Dad out of his office, and we sat at the kitchen table, which is where talks in our family are always held, and he told me the story. He did not seem as shaken up as Mother. It was as though he had been anticipating this moment for a long time.

"I always figured someday we'd have to go through this with you," he said. "Someday something would come up — a need for medical history, maybe — and you couldn't keep thinking your genes were coming straight down the line from the Strattons and the Comptons. The trend today is toward total openness about adoption. Still, that idea has been upsetting to your mother."

"We have such a good life together, the five of us," Mother said defensively. "I couldn't bear to think of spoiling it. Whether its the 'trend' or not, it can't be a good

68

thing to split a family into segments. You hear about all these young people discovering that they're adopted and going off to find their 'real parents,' as though their adoptive parents were nothing more than babysitters."

"I want to know," I said flatly. "I want to know everything."

"Well, I'll tell you," Dad said, "but first I want some wine."

He got up and got glasses for himself and Mother, and would have given me one but I waved it away. Then he sat back down and poured for the two of them and raised his glass and took a swallow.

"It's simple," he said. "We wanted a child, and we couldn't have one. We tried for years. Doctors told us your mother's ovaries weren't functioning properly. They couldn't pinpoint the reason, they just weren't. We tried to adopt in New York State and got turned down flat, which wasn't surprising; an aspiring writer married to an aspiring artist, both on welfare, aren't promising parent material.

"But we wanted a kid; we were that selfish, I guess, and had that much faith in ourselves and in each other. We were sure the lean years were going to give way and one or both of us would eventually make it. What we were afraid of was that by the time that happened we'd be beyond the age to qualify. We heard that there were babies with mixed racial backgrounds available in the Southwest, so we went there. That was the trip we were talking about that night Helen was here."

"Mixed racial backgrounds," I repeated numbly. "What exactly am I?"

"Your natural father was white," Dad said. "Your natural mother was full-blooded Navajo."

69

"I'm half Indian?" I whispered, stunned. "That's why I look the way I do! My hair — my features —"

"Your alien eyes." Dad was trying to make a joke of it, but he couldn't carry it off. He took a deep swig of wine and refilled his glass. "Look at it this way, Laurie — who *isn't* 'mixed racial'? The roots of humanity are so meshed, we're all of us blends and combinations. In all probability, Adam was black and Eve was white."

"That's not funny."

"It's not supposed to be. Who can say it's not true? Is there any place in the Bible where we're told that God Himself isn't part Indian? Honey —" He reached for my hand and looked hurt as I jerked it away. "Laurie, it's not that big a deal. You're the same person you always were. You're our beloved daughter. You're one of us, a Stratton. So what if the same wind that blew the little kids into our lives didn't blow you? You got here. That's what's important."

"If you really felt that way you wouldn't have concealed the truth from me," I said coldly. "Now, I want to know about my twin."

"What's there to know except that you had one?" Dad said. "Your father evidently walked out on your mother at some point during her pregnancy. She gave birth to two babies and knew she wouldn't be able to raise them alone. It was a measure of her love for you that she wanted you to have a better life than she could give you."

"Did you see her?" I asked. "The other baby?"

"Of course. You were there together in the same crib at the agency."

"Did she look exactly like me?"

"You were identical."

"Then, why —" The question rose to my lips without my

even realizing that I was going to ask it. "Why did you take me instead of her?"

"We couldn't raise both of you," Dad said. "We were going out on a limb to take on even one dependent at that point in our lives."

"That's not what I asked," I said. "What I want to know is, why did you choose me over my sister?"

There was a moment's silence as my parents exchanged glances.

Then Dad said slowly, "Your mother — your mother, well, she thought —"

"I didn't want her," Mother said. Her normally gentle voice was strangely sharp. "I just didn't want her. I wanted you."

"But if we were just alike —"

"You weren't alike," Mother said. "You *looked* just alike — both of you so beautiful with big, solemn eyes and all that thick, dark hair. The people at the agency wanted us to take you both, and despite what Dad says, I really think we might have done it. It seemed wrong to separate twin sisters. I picked you up and cuddled you, and I knew I never wanted to let you go. It was as though you were meant to be ours. Then I handed you to Dad to hold and picked up the other baby, and — and —"

"And what?" I prodded.

"I wanted to put her down."

"Why did you want to do that?" I asked in bewilderment.

"That's what Dad kept asking me. I couldn't explain it to him then, and I can't to you now. It was instinctive. She felt alien in my arms. I knew I would not be able to love her."

"Just like that? Without any reason?"

"There was something strange about her. I can't tell you what it was. I know it doesn't make sense. I'm not a baby-lover by nature. There are women who are, you know — women who adore all babies, just because of their babyness — but I've always been selective about the people in my life, babies as well as adults. I even used to wonder, when I was pregnant with Neal, how I would feel about him after he was born, and whether I would be able to love him the way I did you. I could *pick* you. He was an unknown." She smiled slightly. "Of course, that was a ridiculous worry. Neal and Megan were meant to be ours just the way you were."

"How could you have gotten pregnant with the children if your ovaries weren't working?" I asked her, almost accusingly.

"We don't know," Dad said, speaking for her. "The doctors couldn't give us any explanation. Maybe they made a mistake in their diagnosis, or maybe there were chemical changes in your mother's body. Who knows? There again, what does it matter? We're here — we're a family. Now that you know your background, there's nothing left for you to wonder about. Can't we just file this away and go on with our normal lives?"

"It's not that easy," I said. "I want to find my twin."

"This is just what I was afraid of!" exclaimed Mother. "It's the reason I didn't want you to know. You can't just accept it, can you? Oh, no. You've got to want more; you have to find out about these people who aren't anything to you."

"The girl is my sister."

"*Megan* is your sister!"

"Meg is my *adoptive* sister," I said bitterly, accentuating the word. "I want to know about my real, blood sister."

"You're just trying to hurt us." Mother's voice was rising. "You're trying to punish us for not telling you before."

"Easy now, Shelly," Dad said soothingly, laying a restraining hand on her arm. "It's natural for Laurie to react this way. It's a shock to discover there's a part of your past you've not been aware of."

"But now she wants to discard the people who've loved and raised her and go out hunting for perfect strangers!"

"I want to know about my sister," I repeated. How dared my mother put me on the defensive this way, when it was she and Dad who had produced the situation?

"Aren't you even curious about how I came to know about her? It's because she comes to me at night."

"Oh, look now, Laurie —" Dad began.

"You don't believe me? You think I'm lying?"

"I think you're very upset," Dad said.

"Of course, I am. I'm upset because the two people I trusted most in the world have deceived me all my life, and I'm upset because this sister — this Lia — has been visiting me at night, stirring around my dreams, appearing places where people think she's me. Remember, Dad, when you thought you saw me going up to my room, and I wasn't even in the house? That was Lia. She went into my room. She looked through my things. She sat on my bed. When I entered the room later, I could feel her there. Then, when Helen spent the night —"

"Make her stop it, Jim," Mother pleaded. "I can't take any more of this. You see now how right I was, don't you? We never should have told her."

"You wouldn't have if I hadn't forced you," I reminded

73

her. "If you don't believe me about Lia's having been here, how do you think I found out about her?"

"Obviously, you must have gone through the file and found the adoption papers," Dad said. "Get a grip on yourself, Laurie. Overdramatizing isn't going to accomplish anything. Your mother and I feel bad enough about this already. So, you're adopted. So, you're angry because we didn't tell you sooner. All right, then — you're angry. Perhaps you have a right to be. But there's one thing you'll have to admit if you're honest. It's that we love you. Any mistakes we may have made were made for that reason. You don't doubt that, do you?"

I was silent a moment. Then I had to answer, "No."

Furious as I was at them, I did not doubt that they loved me.

CHAPTER 7

AND BECAUSE OF THAT — BECAUSE THEY loved me, and I knew it, and they knew I knew it — we could not stay estranged. We were stiff with each other for a day or so, but that subsided. It was especially hard to remain aloof when the children were around. I looked at Megan, bustling about in that funny, self-important way of hers, and found myself smiling as I always had. And when Neal sat, dreamy-eyed, over his drawings, his soft, pale hair fluffed forward over his forehead, I was filled with the same surge of overwhelming tenderness I had experienced when he was first brought home to Cliff House. These were my sister and brother. Nothing could change that.

And Dad and Mother were my parents.

So we slipped back into what Dad had referred to as "our normal lives." We didn't speak again about my adoption. The only two people I told about it were Gordon and Helen. Gordon didn't say very much, but, then, what was there that he *could* say? He mumbled something about its being "really a wild thing to find out about yourself" and switched the subject as though it embarrassed him.

Helen reacted with no surprise at all.

"I thought that might be it," she said. "Especially after I met your family and saw how blond they were. I even guessed about the Indian heritage. You're lighter-complexioned than the kids I went to school with, but your eyes and those high cheekbones are very much Navajo."

"I can't think of myself as part Indian," I said.

"Of course you can't, because you haven't been raised as one. You feel like a Stratton. But, Lia — who knows about her? She could have been adopted by — well, by *anyone*. She might live here in New England or in California or Florida or anywhere."

"Or even in some foreign country if her adoptive parents were diplomats or something," I said, intrigued by the idea.

"Or she might still be in New Mexico," Helen continued. "The location doesn't make any difference. If she can project herself, she can do it from any place she is."

"But how would she know how?" I asked. "I'd never even heard of astral projection until you explained it to me. How would Lia know about it? And, given that she must, how could she ever have learned to do it?"

"There's one person who can answer that," Helen said.

"And there's no way to ask her. She hasn't come to me since that night you saw her. Maybe she got frightened at finding a stranger in the bed she thought was mine. Maybe she's not coming back."

"I hope that's true," Helen said.

"Oh, no!" The words burst from me without conscious thought, and I was as startled by them as Helen.

76

"But I thought you wanted her gone," she said in surprise.

"I did, but now —" I let the sentence trail off, unsure of how to finish it.

"She's evil, Laurie. She's out to hurt you."

"You can't know that," I countered.

"I saw it in her eyes that night. I *told* you —"

"It was dark, and you were half asleep," I said. "She scared you, appearing at your bedside that way. She didn't do anything to you, though, did she? And she has never hurt me either. She just visits, as though she wants to know about my life. Why shouldn't she, when she's my sister?"

"You used to be frightened of her," Helen said.

"That was before." *We floated together in the same sea before birth.* I had not understood, but now I did. *We are the two sides of a coin.* Suddenly I was filled with a terrible sense of loss. "I want to know about *her* too. There must be some way of locating her. Don't you imagine the adoption agency kept records?"

"Probably," Helen said. "But I can't believe they'd release them to you. Besides, you don't know what agency handled the adoptions."

"My parents do."

"You can't ask them," Helen said. "You know they're not going to tell you. You said your mother freaked out over the thought that you might want to track down your other parents."

"I don't have to ask them," I told her. "I know where to look for what I need."

The information was in the steel filing cabinet in my father's office. It was not difficult to find. And, since Dad had already accused me of having "gone through the file," I

77

did not feel any special guilt about living up to the accusation. I went into the office on a Saturday morning when Dad was still asleep and Mother and Neal were upstairs painting, pulled out the sliding drawers, and riffled through the alphabetically arranged contents.

There were book and movie contracts, business correspondence, bank and royalty statements and packets of research material. There were also folders on each of us children. Ignoring the ones on Neal and Meg, I pulled out the one marked "Laurie." In it I was surprised to find my old grammar school report cards, as well as a collection of hand-drawn birthday and Father's Day cards dating back to kindergarten days. There were also a set of formal papers, proclaiming me legally the child of James and Shelly Stratton, and carbons of several short letters to a "Mrs. Margaret Hastings, Director of Hastings Adoption Agency" in Gallup, New Mexico.

The letters revealed nothing of personal interest; they were confirmations of appointments that had apparently been made by telephone. They did, however, contain the address of the agency. I copied it down, returned the folder to the file, and went up to my room to write the letter. Fifteen minutes later I was on my bicycle, headed for the post office in the village to put it into the mail. The return address I gave was Helen's, as I did not want my parents finding an envelope with an agency letterhead in our postbox.

As it turned out, I need not have worried about that. An answer to my letter did not arrive until the first week of November, and when it did come, it was on the personal stationery of a "Mrs. Thomas Kelsey."

In the meanwhile, autumn moved in upon us. The air became crisp and then chill, and the trees on the mainland turned gold and red. On the island the grasses and sea oats browned. The little scrub oaks lost their leaves, and the poison ivy in the thickets along the sides of the road blazed a brilliant crimson.

By mid-October the prams had been removed from the water, and the only boats to be seen upon the horizon were those of commercial fishermen. The souvenir shops and the art gallery closed, and the streets of the village were void of tourists. The waves curled high on the deserted beaches, and blue days alternated with gray.

Autumn does not last long on Brighton Island. It serves only as a brief prelude to winter.

I was no longer seeing much of Gordon. There were reasons. He and Blane had decided to go out for the basketball team, which meant they had to stay after school for practices and take a later ferry to the island. On weekends he worked with his father doing repair work on some of the summer cottages. The Ahearns owned a group of these on the southern end of the island.

We did attend the Halloween dance at the high school, triple-dating with Blane and Darlene, and Tommy and a girl named Joyce. It should have been fun. The gym had been decorated with pumpkins and corn shucks, and there was a witch on a broomstick silhouetted against a full moon over the dance floor. There was a live band thumping out a beat, and even the chaperons were out there doing their halftime jitterbugs. I just could not get myself into the spirit of the evening. I did all the expected things. I danced and laughed and made party chitchat and gulped the punch that Blane had spiked liberally with vodka from a flask he'd brought in a bag marked "Tricks and Treats."

But something was missing. I felt it, and so did Gordon.

When he brought me home he asked me, "Did you have a nice time?"

"Wonderful," I said. "Did you?"

"Sure," he said. "Great."

It was as though if we kept reassuring ourselves long enough and enthusiastically enough, the words would become true.

On the ferry in the mornings I still rode with Gordon and his crowd, but on the return trips I climbed to the top deck and sat alone or with Neal. The wind there was strong and cold, and I huddled in my ski jacket and kept a muffler pulled across the lower half of my face. Sometimes Jeff was there, hunched over a book, a gloved hand cupped against the bad side of his face to protect it from the wind. When he was, I sat beside him, neither of us talking much. I found his silent company more to my liking than the incessant chatter of the group below.

At school I continued to share lunch with Helen, and one Friday I went home with her to spend the weekend. It was the first time I had had the opportunity to meet her parents. They were much as I had expected, pleasant people who obviously adored their daughter.

"We're concerned about whether we did the right thing by moving here," Mrs. Tuttle confided at dinner. "The cost of living is so much higher, and while Mr. Tuttle was able to find a teaching job, I wasn't, so I'm just substituting. We thought it would be good for Helen to be exposed to another sort of life. She's such an outgoing girl, we never thought for a moment that she'd have problems making friends."

"Helen has friends," I assured her.

"Oh, I know, but except for you they're such casual ones. She never gets asked to parties or to people's houses. Maybe it just takes time. We've all heard stories about that famous New England reserve."

"The boy with the scarred face comes over some," Mr. Tuttle interjected.

"Jeff?" I turned to Helen in surprise. "You didn't tell me that."

"There's nothing to tell," Helen said. "He's been over a few times, and one night we went to the movies. It's no big deal."

"He's a strange young man," her mother said. "He looks almost Satanic. It's tragic what happened to him, and I'm terribly sorry, but it can't do much for Helen's reputation to be seen with him. I'd hate for people to start thinking they were romantically involved."

"I'm not exactly the world's most glamorous creature myself," Helen said lightly. "Who cares what people think? Besides, I like Jeff. His looks don't bother me. He's lonely, and I —" She didn't complete the sentence. To cover the unspoken words, she gave a bright, natural-sounding laugh and shoved her chair back from the table. "Great dinner, Mom! Laurie, do you want to play records?"

There was a lot of pride in Helen Tuttle. Never was I to hear her admit to anyone that her life was not exactly as she would have it, and that she, too, was lonely.

The evening was relaxed and uneventful. We listened to records and watched television (how quiet it was in a house without children!) and by eleven we were in our pajamas. Once settled into the twin bed across from Helen's, I found that I was not at all sleepy. The rattle of traffic in the street outside the Tuttles' two-story town house was an alien sound. I pictured the surf breaking against the rocks beneath the windows of Cliff House and tried to transform the city noises into the roar of waves. The children would be asleep now, and so would Mother. Dad would be settled in his office at the typewriter. My own room would be empty.

Or — would it?

What if Lia has come? I asked myself. What if she is there now, looking for me?

Instantly, I could see her on the screen of my closed lids as she had been that first night, reflected in the glass of the balcony doors. My face. My hair. My features. But the mouth with corners lifted in a secret smile that had not been mine. Myself, yet not myself. The other half of me. Was she now at Cliff House? Somehow, I was sure she was. For so many nights I had lain awake waiting for her, it was fate that it would be on this night that I was not here to receive her that she would come.

Lia! I called silently. Lia, don't go off again!

I reached out for her with my mind, willing my thoughts in her direction. Mentally, I saw myself entering Cliff House and moving up the stairs — past the kitchen — past the darkened living room — past the children's room and my parents' — to my own bedroom door. I stretched out my hand and rested it upon the knob. She was there. I could feel her on the far side, resting quiet, waiting. I knew it, but I was powerless to reach her. The knob would not turn.

"Helen?" I whispered. "Are you awake?"

"Mmmmmm." There was the sound of her body shifting beneath the blankets in the bed across from me.

"I need to ask you something." I hoisted myself up onto my elbow. "Helen, do you think I could do it too?"

"Do what?" The urgency in my voice must have gotten through to her, because she no longer sounded sleepy. "What is it you're thinking of doing?"

"Projecting. I'm identical to Lia. Isn't it logical that whatever mind power she has would be available to me? A moment ago I was thinking about Cliff House, and I had this feeling that if I tried hard enough, if I could just figure how to direct myself, I could will myself there!"

"No!" Helen said sharply. "You must never try!"

"Why shouldn't I?" I was becoming more and more excited by the idea. "Think what it could mean! If I could free myself from my body the way Lia does, I could do anything! I could travel anywhere!"

"Don't talk that way, Laurie. I don't want to listen."

"But, why?" I asked reasonably.

"Because it's unnatural."

"In the Indian world it isn't. You told me that yourself."

"You're not in the Indian world," Helen said. "It doesn't matter about your heritage. You haven't been trained in this. You'd be messing around with something you don't know how to handle." There was a note of real panic in her voice. "It's dangerous. You have no idea what might end up happening. I want you to promise you won't even try."

"Then you believe it would be possible that I could learn?"

"I guess it's possible," Helen said reluctantly. "But if you do, I just know that you'll be sorry."

"I don't understand why you're so scared by the idea." I settled back on the pillow. My heart was pounding. "You talked about it so matter-of-factly when it was Luis's father. If he could project himself to watch the birth of his son, why shouldn't I do the same thing to find my sister? She's somewhere in the world, a living person, not just a mirror girl. I could go to her the same way she has to me."

"There are better ways," Helen said. "You've written the adoption agency. Any day now you're going to hear from them. Maybe they'll send you an address. Then you could write or phone her."

"I don't think they're going to answer," I told her. "It's been almost a month now. And if they do, you yourself said they might not be willing to tell me anything."

"Give them a chance," Helen pleaded. "Give them a little more time. They might come through. We can't be sure. Please, believe me, it would be so much better a way." She paused, and when I did not respond she continued, "Promise me, Laurie. I want to hear you say it."

"All right," I agreed reluctantly. "I promise. I'll wait a little longer."

The letter arrived three days later. Helen brought it to school, and I read it standing in a stall in the girls' restroom. It was the only privacy I could find.

The writer, Mrs. Kelsey, was the daughter of Margaret Hastings.

"Your letter was forwarded here to Phoenix," she wrote me. "The agency was closed after my mother's death. The records are sealed and have been placed in storage. I do recollect that there was once a case in which there were twins to place. It was an unusual enough occurrence so that my mother used to talk about it. She was disappointed that they could not have been placed together. One child was adopted, and the other was reclaimed by her mother. Some years later the mother died, and the child was again brought to the agency. I believe she was placed in a foster home.

"I'd advise you not to concern yourself further with this matter. I'm sure you have a good home. Let the past stay buried, and enjoy your present. I am sure that is what your sister is doing."

But I knew better. I folded the letter and placed it in my purse.

The following week, Lia returned to Brighton Island. But not to me.

CHAPTER 8

I LEARNED ABOUT HER FROM JEFF.

"You shouldn't go walking around out on those rocks by your house," he told me. "They're slick as hell."

We were standing at the railing on the top deck of the ferry with Neal wedged between us, and the wind whipped the words from his mouth as soon as they were spoken. I was not sure he had said what I thought he had.

"I never walk there," I told him across the top of my brother's head.

"You did yesterday," Jeff insisted. "I saw you."

"We never walk out there," said Neal, echoing my words. "Not any of us. It's dangerous. I fell once when I was a little kid and almost got killed."

"You're darned right, it's dangerous," Jeff said. "Those rocks have crevices between them. One little slip, and you've had it."

My mind had stopped several sentences back at the words "I saw you." It was like a replay of the scene with Natalie and Gordon on the day after Nat's party. There was no way

Jeff could have seen me on the rocks by Cliff House. I had not been there.

I gazed out across the water at the dark shape of Brighton Island growing larger and larger as we approached it. The girl on the rocks had been Lia. About that there was no question in my mind. Somewhere up ahead, on the rocks or beaches or cliffs, or even more likely in the quiet sanctuary of Cliff House itself, she was waiting. Soon now I would find her.

But this did not occur. I went to bed early that night, tense with anticipation, and lay awake until dawn. When the outline of the bedroom furniture became visible, and the sky beyond the glass doors went from black to gray and softened into pink, I finally closed my eyes. Disappointment accentuated my exhaustion, and I slept like a dead thing for the hour that was left before Meg was sent to wake me.

She has gone again, I told myself. But once more I was wrong. That afternoon when Neal returned from his usual after-school wanderings he seemed surprised to find me in the living room reading.

"I thought I saw you out on the dunes," he said. "I was riding my bike down Star Point Road toward the cranberry bogs, and there was this girl up at the top of one of the sandhills. The sun was behind her, but I was sure it was you."

Meg, who was occupied in leading a group of stuffed animals through a third grade spelling lesson, glanced up with interest.

"I bet it was Laurie's ghosty again," she said.

"What do you mean?" Neal asked.

"There's this ghost thing that goes around peeking at

people. I see her all the time. At first I thought it was Laurie, but now I know different."

"That's crazy," Neal said disdainfully. "There's no such things as ghosts, and if there were, they wouldn't come out in the daytime, and they wouldn't belong to live people."

"This one does," said Megan.

Neal, finding the subject too ridiculous to argue about, went off to the kitchen to ransack the refrigerator. As soon as he was gone, I turned upon my sister.

"Did you really mean that, about seeing this — this ghost person — more than that one time when you thought it was me looking in your window?"

"Sure," Megan said. "Sometimes she goes by in the hall. Neal's bed is over against the wall, so he can't see out the door the way I can. She looks in at us, but she doesn't stop. She goes on up the stairs."

It was more than I could take. Here I was reaching for Lia — trying with all my strength to make contact — with no success, while my brother and sister and even someone as remote from my life as Jeff Rankin were seeing her everywhere. What could be the reason? Was I trying too hard and in some way establishing a block to communication? Or did Lia simply not want me to find her? If that were the case, why would she be coming here at all? Surely she must mean for me to know of her continued existence, or she would not move where the others could see her. It was as though she were playing some cat-and-mouse game with me, filling my ears with elusive whispers of her presence, but keeping herself always out of sight.

With a sigh, I got up from my seat on the sofa and went over to the window. The sun was low in the sky and shielded by a thin layer of clouds so that the world was awash with cold, gray light. The water looked dull and flat with a metallic cast that gave it the illusion of solidity. I could almost imagine some adventurous soul attempting to walk across it to the mainland. Off to the west I could see the chunky shape of the ferry making its late afternoon trip back to the island with its load of office workers and those high school students who had stayed for meetings and sports activities.

Gordon would be on that ferry. Suddenly I wanted nothing in the world so much as to be there with him on the deck of the bow. I was tired of worrying, tired of wondering, tired of the emotional exhaustion the past few months had brought upon me. I wanted to fly back in time and circumstance to those fine, fair summer days when life had been so simple and I had been no one and nothing except Laurie Stratton, secure in my identity, secure in my relationships, with nothing more to fill my mind than sunning and sailing and falling in love.

I turned abruptly away from the window.

"I'm going out for a little while," I said to Megan.

"I wouldn't," she said. "You know, it's got really cold outside."

I regarded her with astonishment. "Are you playing mother?"

"I don't think you ought to go out there," she said. "That ghost thing is on the dunes. Neal said so."

"That 'ghost thing' is anywhere she wants to be," I said crisply. "From what you tell me, she's around this house more than anyplace else. She hasn't hurt anyone yet, has she?"

"I'm not scared of her here," Meg said. "Not when we're all of us together. Out there it's different. You'll be by yourself, and she might not let you come back."

"You let me worry about that," I told her. "Actually, I'd love to run into the 'ghosty,' as you call her. There are a lot of things I want to ask her. In the meantime, I'm going down to the pier and meet the ferry. Maybe I'll bring Gordon back with me."

I left my young sister surrounded by her animals, all of whom seemed to be staring after me with worried glass eyes. At the bottom of the stairway I got my jacket out of the coat closet and opened the front door and stepped out into the cold.

Megan had been right about the temperature. It had taken a sudden drop in the latter part of the day, as though to keep pace with the graying of the water and sky. The air had the smell and feel of approaching rain. I zipped my jacket up to the collar and thrust my hands deep into its pockets and started down the Beach Road toward the landing.

The passenger load on the Brighton Island Ferry changes greatly after Labor Day weekend. During the summer months the boat is jammed on the 5:15 run from the island back to the mainland. There are crying babies and sandy, salty children and weary parents clutching diaper bags and picnic baskets and empty thermoses that started the day filled with Kool-Aid. They crowd the dock, shoving and snapping and nursing their sunburns in feverish concern that if they are not the first on board they will be left behind. In the winter it's different. Daytime visitors to the island are few. When I reached the pier the only one waiting there was Mary Beth Ziegler.

"Hi," I said, sitting down beside her on the plank bench by the seawall. "Are you going somewhere or are you meeting someone?"

"Neither, exactly. Mom sent me down to bring my dad's dinner." She gestured toward the tin dinner pail which she had set on the ground between her feet. "What about you?"

"I'm meeting Gordon," I said. "He stayed after school for practice."

"Darlene waits in the afternoons for Blane so they can ride back together."

"She must really like basketball."

"Darlene likes *Blane.*" There was a moment's silence. Then Mary Beth said carefully, "On that subject, she felt really hurt about your not showing on Saturday. Even if you couldn't make it, you might have sent over a present or a card."

"A present?" I said. "Why?"

"It's expected on birthdays. Especially when there's a party."

"Was Saturday Darlene's birthday?"

"Oh, Laurie, come off it," Mary Beth said irritably. "Of course, it was her birthday. Nat and I gave her a surprise slumber party and I invited you myself. If you couldn't come, you might have called me."

"You invited me?" My voice came out thin and strange, rising into a squeak at the end of the question. I drew a deep breath and forced it into control. "I'm afraid you're wrong. You may have meant to ask me, but you didn't. I didn't know a thing about the party."

"I certainly did ask you," Mary Beth said firmly. "That day last week when it got so foggy. You were out in front of the post office when I was coming out with the mail."

"And I said I'd come?"

"You sure didn't say you wouldn't. You smiled and nodded. I was in a hurry — Ren was waiting with the car — and I thought you'd call me if you wanted more details. Don't tell me you don't remember."

"I don't," I said. "I'm sorry. I must have been thinking about something else and not heard you. It was the day of the fog?"

There had been such a day. Fog is common on the island in November. The mists rise from the water, and when the sun doesn't break through the clouds to burn them off, they settle upon the village like a blanket. It had been on Wednesday — no, on Thursday. And where had I been? Did I go into the village for the mail that day? It was certainly possible.

No — I hadn't been there; suddenly, I remembered. Mother had been crating some oils Thursday for a show in Boston. Crating paintings was always a family project, and I had gone straight home after school to help. The fog had been thick on the Beach Road, and I had not been able to see Cliff House until I reached it. Then it had appeared directly in front of me, as though a curtain had been jerked away to reveal it. I had entered and climbed the stairs to the living room and gone directly to the window. It had been like standing in the middle of a cloud. I had not even been able to see the water.

No, on Thursday I had not been in the village.

"You heard me," Mary Beth was saying. "I was just a couple of feet away from you, and you looked right at me."

"I said I'm sorry," I told her.

"Being sorry won't cut it. It's just not enough. You're going to have to do something about yourself, Laurie.

You've changed so much since last summer. Everybody's noticing. You're like a different person. Nat says she bets your folks may be getting divorced or something."

"Nat says *what?*" I exclaimed.

"Well, maybe they're not, but it wouldn't be a surprise to anybody. People who shut themselves away like they do are usually having problems. If that's the case, it would explain why you're acting so withdrawn and funny lately. Nat says —"

"I don't give a damn what Nat says!" I exploded. "My parents are very happy, thank you. A divorce is the last thing in the world they're considering. Nat and the rest of you have a lot of nerve! My parents' personal life is their own business!"

"Laurie, calm down, please." Mary Beth looked nervous. "I didn't mean to get you all upset. Gordon had said something to Nat about — well, about how you'd found out something that had stirred things up between you and your folks. He didn't tell her what it was. We just assumed —"

"You have no right to assume anything," I said angrily. "And as for Gordon —"

"Don't be mad at Gordon," Mary Beth said. "He was trying to make excuses for you, that's all." She got to her feet and bent to pick up the dinner pail. "Here comes the boat. I've got to take this down and give it to Dad."

I got up too. I was shaking with anger. My hands were balled into fists in the pockets of my jacket. I had confided in Gordon! I had trusted him! And he had turned right around and spilled everything out to strangers! He had told them — but, no, in fairness I had to concede that he hadn't told them about my adoption; if he had, Mary Beth would

93

certainly have mentioned that. And these weren't strangers. They were my friends as well as Gordon's, or at least they were supposed to be. It was not their fault that I had drawn away from them. As Mary Beth had said, it was I who had changed since the previous summer, when I had been thrilled to be included in their every activity. Mary Beth, Natalie, Gordon — they were just the same now as they had always been. If they were looking for answers to explain my own odd behavior, that was understandable.

"Mary Beth," I said. "Wait a minute."

She had started down the pier. Now she turned to glance back at me.

"What is it?"

"I'm sorry," I said for the third time. "Really. I'd have liked to have gone to the party. I've had things on my mind, but they haven't had anything to do with my parents' marriage."

"I'm glad," Mary Beth said coolly. "I hope you get the 'things' — whatever they are — worked out." Her mouth had a tight, pursed look to it, as though to make clear to me that people didn't get mad and raise their voices to the likes of Mary Beth Ziegler.

She turned her back and started again down the pier. I recalled suddenly the day I had brought Helen to the island table in the school cafeteria. Mary Beth's mouth had condensed itself in the same way then.

I didn't feel like trailing her down to the boat, so I stood where I was and watched it from a distance. This was what Megan always referred to as the "coming home ferry," because most of the people arriving on it had homes on the island but worked on the mainland. The men in business suits and overcoats came trooping off, carrying their briefcases, and behind them came Blane and Darlene, walking arm in arm. I knew I probably should intercept them and make my apologies. After all, it was Darlene's birthday celebration that I had not attended. I toyed with the idea and then discarded it. I just wasn't ready to go through another confrontation.

I expected Gordon to disembark directly behind them, but he didn't. It wasn't until several minutes later that I saw him emerging from the cabin, and a girl was with him. They crossed the deck together, so deep in conversation that they kept walking into people. When Gordon stepped onto the dock, he turned back and took the girl's hand to help her across.

It was Joyce, Tommy Burbank's date from the Halloween dance. She was a sophomore, if I remembered correctly — little, blonde, and giggly. She was giggling now, with her head tipped back so that her eyes would twinkle up at Gordon, who was making this easy by bending over her. They came on slowly up the dock, Hansel-and-Greteling along with their clasped hands swinging between them, and passed within six feet of me without noticing.

So — good-bye to Gordon.

I spoke the words silently. What would happen, I wondered, if I shouted them after him? Would the sound of my voice cause those hands to loose their hold on each other and go flying apart? Would Gordon whirl and come rushing back to greet me, redfaced and stammering?

"Laurie! I didn't see you there! This is Joyce — remember Joyce? She was over at the school watching practice, and she forgot her gloves, and I was just trying to —"

No, that wouldn't be Gordon. He didn't take guilt trips.

"Look, Laurie," he would say defensively, "you've been

acting so weird, I thought you'd just as soon I found somebody else to spend my time with. Now you can be free to concentrate on whatever the hell it is you're so wrapped up in lately."

Having once heard the words in my head, I felt no need to hear them spoken. So I stood there, quiet, watching Gordon and Joyce walk away together, surprised that I was feeling so little. I should have been hurt, shouldn't I? My first real love was mine no longer. I should, at the very least, have been angry.

Good-bye to Gordon. Good-bye to green eyes that told me I was pretty and to sun-bleached hair, warm beneath my fingers. Good-bye to the mouth that taught me how to kiss.

Why wasn't I crying? Why was I feeling nothing? Where was the pain, the agony of loss I'd read so much about? Such a short time before I'd longed for Gordon. I'd come to the dock to meet him — expecting what? That I could go back again? That I could be a person I was no longer?

As the last of the departing passengers moved up the pier, I fell into step with them.

"It's going to be a cold winter," the man walking next to me commented conversationally as the chill wind swept upon us from across the water.

"You're right about that," I told him.

I took my north turn on the Beach Road, and when the dunes cut off the wind the cold did not seem to lessen as one might have expected, but in some strange way it grew more intense. I should have been shivering, but I wasn't. It was as though I were a part of the cold and therefore could not react to it. Ice within ice. Numbness all the way through to the emptiness at my core.

Eventually, I began to realize that I was no longer alone.

She was beside me. Lia.

We continued on in silence, the two of us, shoulder to shoulder, with the night descending upon us thick and fast the way it does in winter. I did not turn to look at her until we were nearly to Cliff House. It was enough to know that she was there.

When the curve of the road brought us into view of the house, I did turn.

"Hello," I said.

"Hello to you." She regarded me solemnly. The eyes, grave and questioning, set in my own familiar face. My own voice coming soft to me through the semidarkness. "You are ready?"

"I've been waiting and waiting," I said accusingly.

"I know, but you weren't yet ready. Now you are."

We went up the path and entered Cliff House together. And together we remained.

CHAPTER 9

WE ARE THE TWO SIDES OF A COIN.

Lia and I.

When I say we remained together, I don't mean, of course, that she was there in reality through every moment of the day and night. She had her other plane of existence about which she refused to be questioned. She came and went, yet even when I was alone I felt her continuing presence. She had moved now from my dreams into my everyday world, a shadow sliding across my plate at dinner, a whisper grown so loud that it drowned out the sound of other voices.

"You haven't been listening to anything Meg's been saying," my father accused me.

"Of course, I have."

"About her story —"

"I was listening to it."

"I wasn't *telling* a story, I was saying how I *wrote* one," Megan informed me in a hurt voice. "They're going to print it in the school paper."

"That's great," I said. "It really is."

There was a moment's silence.

"Laurie," Dad said slowly, "are you all right? You just don't seem like yourself lately."

"I'm fine. Just fine."

I'd leave the table after dinner at night, do the dishes, and gather up my books as though I were going to study. No lingering with the family. No silly card games. I'd climb the stairs to my room, where Lia might be waiting, and, if she were not, then I would be the one to wait.

"What does she do up there every evening?" my father asked, his voice floating up to me from the living room below. "She can't have that much homework all of a sudden. She's never spent time in her room like this before."

"She's seventeen," Mother reminded him. "That's a difficult age. I think she must have had a fight with Gordon. He hasn't been phoning the way he used to."

"He's got a new girlfriend," volunteered Megan, the walking newspaper.

"Oh, dear," said Mother. "Poor Laurie! She must feel terrible. I wouldn't be that age again for anything in the world. Everything hurts so terribly."

Her sympathy gave me a twinge of guilt, for I did not deserve it. The truth was that I could probably have worked things out with Gordon. He had come up to me at school the day after I had seen him on the pier, ready, I think, to make amends.

"Mary Beth says you went down to the boat to meet me yesterday," he began a little nervously. "I didn't see you there."

"I know you didn't."

"And now you're mad because you saw me talking to Joyce?"

"I'm not mad," I said. "There's no need for you to explain anything."

"Joyce stayed after school with Darlene," Gordon said. "They're real good friends. Darlene always stays to watch practice and ride back with Blane, and Joyce was with her. We came back across on the same ferry."

"Hand in hand?"

"I took her hand to help her get ashore. You can't be jealous about something like that, Laurie. If you'd ever take the time to stay for practices like other girls do when the guys they go with are on the team —"

"I said, I'm not mad," I interrupted.

"The hell you're not!"

"I'm really not," I assured him levelly. "I was a little upset at first, I guess, but I've gotten over it. I think it's nice that you and Joyce have found each other. Like you've told me before, things between you and me aren't the way they used to be. If they were, I *would* be watching practices."

Gordon stared at me, incredulous — more startled, I think, by my lack of emotion than by the words themselves. I stared back at him, surprised myself by the fact that I could let the whole thing go so easily when it had once meant so much.

But I was another person now. I had nothing to invest in Gordon. Everything within me was channeled toward Lia.

I would like to be able to explain what it was like with me during that time. I wish I could put it into writing, that strange feeling of being consumed and enveloped by another being. But I am not my father's blood daughter, as Megan is. I do not have his gift with words.

Perhaps I could say that it was a bit like falling in love. When I first started going with Gordon, he was all I could think about. I got up in the morning with his name on my lips — "Gordon — Gordon — today I will see Gordon!" — and I fell asleep at night with his face superimposed upon the inside of my closed lids. Now it was Lia's face — *my* face — that filled my consciousness. What I was experiencing was, in a way, like falling in love with myself.

What was I thinking and feeling back last November on those long evenings when I sat here with Lia, my sister? I can remember the things that were said, but I cannot remember our voices. I can remember the fact of her presence — the curve of her lips, the tilt of her head, the stillness of her. But did I see her with my eyes or with my mind? Was she, in truth, there by the window, or was the sight of her an illusion, something I saw because I wanted so desperately to see it?

I ask this now, because as I am thinking back, I believe that there were times when the room lights were not on. Yet, still, I saw her.

"Tell me," I said, "about our mother."

"She was beautiful," said Lia. "Very slender, with long black hair and quiet eyes. And she never smiled."

"Why not?" I asked.

"Because the world had been cruel to her," Lia said, and she told me the story, making it far and sad like some sort of fairy tale from another place and time. I cannot recall the exact words she used, but I can remember the story itself.

There was once a young Navajo girl, Lia said, so lovely

that all the men in her village wanted to wed her, and she was married at the age of thirteen to the son of the Chief. So, without having known girlhood, she settled down to being a wife. Then one day when she was seventeen, the same age we were now, a trader came through the village in a pickup truck buying turquoise and silver jewelry. He was handsome and fair-complexioned with hair the color of sunshine, and the girl took one look at him and fell violently in love. He asked her to come away with him. She told him that was impossible. But suddenly, when she realized that he was really leaving, she climbed into the cab beside him and rode away with him, leaving everything she owned behind in her husband's hogan.

"I belong to you now," she told the trader. "I will love you and stay beside you until the day I die."

But the trader was a casual man who was used to willing girls and good times, and after several months with his Indian maiden he grew tired of her.

"Go back to your people," he said. "That's where you belong."

"I can't," the girl told him. "My husband would never take me back. Besides, I am going to bear your child."

"That's your problem, not mine," said the trader.

She thought he was joking. But that night he did not come home to her. She sat for three days in their apartment, waiting, until finally she had to realize that he had left her. In the top drawer of his bureau she found an envelope with money in it and a note that told her to put the baby up for adoption. Enclosed was the address of the Hastings Agency.

The "baby" turned out to be twin girls with the trader's fine features. They had lighter skin than their mother's, but had inherited her hair and eyes. Obeying the instructions in the note, the young mother took them to the agency, but because they were of mixed blood they were classified as "hard to place."

"Won't your family help you raise them?" the director, Mrs. Hastings, asked. "The Navajo people always take care of their own."

The girl explained that she could not return to the reservation with half-breed children.

"The people would drive me out," she said. "I am married to the son of the Chief."

So Mrs. Hastings agreed to try to find homes for the babies. There was a couple arriving that week from New York City, a writer married to an artist. They could not qualify as adoptive parents in their own state and were anxious to adopt in the Southwest. They might be persuaded to take the twins.

But this couple decided to take only one of the babies.

"I don't understand it," Mrs. Hastings told the mother. "At first I was certain they were going to want them both. Then, after holding them, the woman seemed to change her mind."

Months passed, and no adoptive family turned up for the second twin. So the mother reclaimed her tiny daughter and set out to attempt to raise her alone.

"Where did you live?" I asked Lia.

"In one low-cost apartment complex after another."

"And *how* did you live? Did your father send support money?"

"Never that I know of. Our mother worked cleaning houses."

"Like Mrs. DeWitt?" Plump, round-shouldered Edna DeWitt came out from the village on Thursdays to do the windows and floors and bathrooms at Cliff House. Mother called her "the greatest thing that's happened since instant coffee."

"Who?" Lia asked, seemingly puzzled.

"The lady who cleans for us," I explained. I had never questioned the fact that Mrs. DeWitt made her living by cleaning houses, but then, she was not by any stretch of the imagination the wife-of-the-son-of-a-Chief. A woman with that title should certainly not be on her knees scrubbing other people's toilet bowls.

"She would take me with her into all those beautiful homes," Lia told me, "and then at the end of the day we would go back to our apartment. We would eat and go to bed. There was nothing else to do in the evening." She could recall, she told me, how in summer the light would slant through the cracks in the blinds for hours after her bedtime. The heat would be heavy in the room, and her pillow would be drenched with sweat. On the ceiling of one of the apartments they lived in, there had been a fan. It had moved slowly around, stirring the heat into lazy waves. Lia would lie on her back and stare up at the revolving blades and feel those waves rolling over her and would pretend they were green and cool like the ocean.

"You had seen the ocean?" I asked in surprise.

"No, but our mother had. She told me about it. She went there many times to search."

"To search for what?"

"For the trader, of course," Lia responded. Was she

irritated at my stupidity or at something else? I felt the vibrations of anger, but I could not assess them. "She had sworn to remain beside him."

"But if she was taking care of you and working every day, when did she ever have the chance?"

"At night. She would stretch herself on the bed across from me, and then she would — *go.*"

"Oh," I said with a rush of understanding. "The way you come here."

"At first I would hear her breathing, slow and heavy," Lia said. "Then everything would go still. It would happen. She would be gone. Sometimes I would turn on the light by the bed and stand looking down at the shell of her, lying there so beautiful and quiet. Her chest would not be moving. I would place my fingers under her nostrils, and I could feel no breath.

"In the morning when I woke she would be back. She would fix us breakfast, and while I ate she would tell me where she had been."

"Where did she go?" I could feel myself, the small Lia, so terribly alone there by my mother's bedside.

"It was usually to California," said Lia. "The trader had told her once that he wanted to go there. Indian jewelry was in demand on the Coast, and the people had money to spend for it. She went from city to city. She could move so quickly that distance made no problem. She was sure that she would find him."

"And did she?" I breathed, so caught in the story that it had become my own.

"I suppose so," said Lia. "There came a day when she did not return."

"And, you? What of *you?* Where are you now?"

To that there was never an answer.

I try now to recall that time, and it is like attempting to remember something that occurred in a dream. You know you did and said certain things that seemed reasonable to you then, but in the light of day, they appear otherwise. In looking back, I realize that I was not in touch with reality. I was living at Cliff House with my family, but whole days would go by when I was hardly aware of their existence.

My parents were worried. I could see it in their faces and hear it in their voices.

"Breaking up with a boyfriend isn't the end of the world, honey," Mother told me. "You learn from the experience. When the right person for you comes along, you'll be better able to love him for having had a chance to practice first."

My father was less gentle.

"Pull yourself together," he said. "When the girls in my novels get broken hearts, I allow them exactly one week to mend. Then, if they're still mooning around, I bring in a monster from outer space to put them out of their misery."

"I'm not 'mooning,' " I told him. "I was as responsible for the breakup as Gordon."

I could tell by his eyes that he did not believe me.

At school I was unable to keep my mind on my classes. I daydreamed through them, and wandered through the halls as though I were in a foreign country. My grades slipped from their usual A's to B's, and from B's to C's. In algebra I pulled the first D of my life.

Some of my teachers were concerned. Others were merely irritated.

"It's too early in the year for senior slump," my algebra teacher remarked crisply.

I could do nothing but nod in agreement. There was no excuse I could offer. How could I have explained that on those evenings when I was supposed to have been studying I had been meeting with the astral image of my sister?

The one person I could talk to was Helen. She was the receptacle into which I poured all my new-found information, the sounding board upon which I bounced the strange thoughts that were a constant tangle in my mind. I expected her to respond with the same wonder and excitement I was experiencing.

Instead, she seemed decidedly unenthusiastic.

"It's not good for you to get so wrapped up in this," she said. "Like Mrs. Kelsey said in her letter, it's a part of your life that's over. Actually, it never touched you. You were only a couple of weeks old when the Strattons adopted you. Whatever went on with Lia and her mother is part of their history, not yours."

"That woman was as much my mother as Lia's," I said stiffly. "Of course, what happened to her is important to me. The whole thing's like a romantic novel with a beautiful, abandoned woman searching the world over for the man she loves."

"I don't find it romantic," Helen said. "I think it's sad and foolish."

"What do you mean?"

"A woman leaves her husband for another man, gets pregnant, and gets dumped," Helen said flatly. "It happens all the time. To me the real love story is your adoptive parents."

"It's no put-down to them if I'm interested in my other family," I said defensively. "Lia's my twin. She's closer to me than anyone in the world."

"You don't know a thing about her," Helen said.

"How can you say that? I know myself, don't I? We're identical."

"In looks," Helen said. "But not in other ways. Your mother sensed a difference. That's why she chose to adopt only one of you. I felt it too that night I spent at Cliff House."

"You're jealous," I accused her. "You don't want me to have a closer friend than you."

It was a cruel thing to say. I could see the hurt flash deep in Helen's eyes, but she kept her voice steady.

"Maybe that's true," she admitted. "It's more than that, though. I'm scared for you, Laurie. You're in this too deep. It's dangerous."

That was Friday.

Saturday I slept late. It was ten-fifteen when Mother came to wake me and to tell me that Helen was in critical condition at Saint Joseph's Hospital.

CHAPTER 10

LEAVING DAD TO STAY WITH THE CHILDREN, Mother and I caught the eleven o'clock ferry across to the mainland. From the pier we took a taxi to the hospital.

The traffic was heavy, and the sidewalks were crowded with bustling hordes of holiday shoppers. I stared out at them through the dirty window of the cab, feeling as though I were waking from a dream. I had been so absorbed with my own concerns that I had totally lost track of the fact that Christmas was approaching. Now, suddenly, it surrounded us. Strings of bright colored lights crisscrossed the main streets of town, and bearded Salvation Army Santas jangled their bells on corners. Carols blared gaily from loudspeakers, and in the lobby of Saint Joseph's Hospital a gigantic fir tree glowed resplendent in red bows and striped candy canes.

We checked at the information desk and then took the elevator to the fifth floor. The first person we saw when the doors drew open was Jeff Rankin. He sat slouched in a chair across from the elevators, looking as though he had molded himself to his seat and taken root there. His eyes had the glitter that comes from lack of sleep. I wondered how long he had been there and how he had learned about Helen so much before I had.

"How is she?" I asked him by way of greeting.

"Not good." He did not seem surprised to see us. "She's been unconscious ever since they brought her in at seven this morning." He paused. "Her folks are over there in a sort of waiting room across from Intensive Care. They let them go in and look at her for five minutes every hour."

"Oh, Lord," Mother said softly. "How terrible."

She put her arm around me, and we walked together down the corridor to the door Jeff had indicated. It stood open. The Tuttles were the only ones in the little room, sitting side by side on a brown leather sofa.

When I had met them my reaction had been that they were young to have a daughter who was a high school senior. I could no longer say that. They looked today as though they had aged a million years.

Mrs. Tuttle's eyes were red from weeping. It seemed to take her a moment to recognize me, and then she said, "Oh — it's Laurie" in an expressionless voice.

"I phoned the Strattons a couple of hours ago," Mr. Tuttle told her. "I thought Helen's best friend should be told before she learned about it from the papers or a news report on the radio. You were good to come, Laurie." His eyes moved past me. "Is this your mother?"

"Yes, I'm Shelly Stratton," Mother said before I could make introductions. "I'm so terribly sorry about Helen's accident. She's such a warm, lovely person. She just *has* to be all right."

"Keep thinking that way," Mr. Tuttle said. "Think positive. That's about all any of us can do right now. She's got good doctors. They're doing everything they can for her. And she's a strong girl. If she weren't she'd never have survived the exposure."

"What exactly happened?" I asked hesitantly. "Mother said you didn't tell her much — just that Helen fell and hit her head."

"We don't even know that, really," Mr. Tuttle said. "It seems the only thing that could have happened, but, of course, she hasn't been able to tell us anything. A man who was taking a shortcut on his way to work found her this morning in the little park across the street from our town house. To think she'd been there all night and we didn't know it! She could have died there, a hundred yards away from us."

"What was she doing in the park at night?" I asked. "That doesn't sound like Helen."

"She was with that boy," Mrs. Tuttle said. It was her first contribution to the discussion, and her voice shrilled unnaturally. "That creepy boy. They went out together last night, and Helen never came back. He was with her. He was responsible."

"Jeff wasn't with her in the park," Helen's father said gently.

"How can we know that? How can we know anything until Helen gets well enough to tell us?" The dull, dead look was gone from her face now, and it was contorted with pain. "All we do know is that Jeff Rankin took our Helen out at seven-thirty and at half past midnight, when she hadn't come home, you called out to the island. Jeff was there. He was in the shower, his father said. When he called back a few minutes later, he said that he'd left Helen all by herself downtown."

"He didn't just 'leave her,' " Mr. Tuttle said. "He put her in a taxi."

"Then why was she in the park? Laurie's right. There's no reason Helen would go into the park alone at that ungodly hour of the night. Girls don't do that. Girls don't jump out of taxicabs in front of their houses and go running off somewhere else. If it was true, what Jeff said — if he did send her home in a taxi — then she would have paid the driver and come directly into the house."

"We can't question her reasons right now," Mr. Tuttle said. "We know that she *did* go into the park and something happened to her there. From what the police tell us, she slipped on an icy path and struck her head on one of the iron benches. At any rate" — he directed himself to Mother and me — "she didn't come home. When it got to be twelve-thirty I phoned out to the Rankins'. Jeff said he'd put Helen into a cab at around eleven and given her money to pay for it. That meant she should have been home by eleven-thirty at the latest."

"Oh, you poor people," Mother said in a low voice. "What you must have gone through."

"We called the police, of course," Mr. Tuttle said. "They came out to the house and took Helen's description and all that. Then they sent a patrol boat to pick up Jeff. Everything they did took such a long time. It seemed like they weren't even worried. One policeman had the gall to suggest that Helen had run away. 'She's that age,' he told us. 'We get reports like this all the time. Usually it turns out the girl's had a fight with her folks or her boyfriend and just wants to shake people up a little.'"

"If only it had been that," Mrs. Tuttle broke in, "but we knew it wasn't. Helen would never hurt us that way. And that boy is *not* her *boyfriend.*"

"They were in the middle of interrogating Jeff when one of the squad cars radioed in," Mr. Tuttle continued as though he had not been interrupted. "Some man, a cook in a coffeehouse over east of where we live, had found Helen. He said he almost fell over her. She was lying unconscious by the side of the path, and her legs were sticking out across it. She'd been there all night in the cold."

He drew a deep breath, and his wife reached over and touched his hand. Now it was she who was trying to give comfort.

"She'll be okay," she said. "We've got to believe that. God wouldn't have let her make it this far if He were going to turn right around and snatch her away from us."

There was a moment's silence. Then I asked, "May I see her?"

"I'm sorry, they've restricted that to family," Mr. Tuttle said. "Just her mother and me for a couple of minutes every hour. Not that it means much. We stand there and look at her and go out again. If they did allow you in, she wouldn't know you were there."

But *I* would know it, I thought miserably. I could tell her that I'm sorry, even if she couldn't hear me. I'm sorry about her accident. I'm sorry I was so horrid to her yesterday.

Suddenly there seemed to be nothing left to say.

"You will call us, won't you, the moment there's any

change?" Mother asked. "We're so concerned — not just Laurie, but all of us."

"Of course, we'll call as soon as there's anything to report." Mr. Tuttle got to his feet. "Thank you both for coming. It means a lot to know there's somebody around here who cares."

"That boy," Mrs. Tuttle said. "Is he still out there?"

"Jeff?" Mother said. "Yes, he's out in the hall. We talked to him briefly on our way in."

"He shouldn't be here. He doesn't have any right." Her voice was sharp. "If it hadn't been for him, this would never have happened."

"Dear — don't —" her husband began.

"Stop telling me 'Don't.' I'm only saying what's a fact. He took Helen out and didn't bring her home again. If he cared about her he would have taken care of her. And now here he is when it's too late, shoving himself in on us like he belonged here."

"He didn't 'shove himself in,'" Mr. Tuttle protested mildly. "I phoned him myself, and the police brought him over from the island."

"But that's over now. He's talked with us; he's talked with them. Why doesn't he leave? Aren't we upset enough? Why did Helen go out with him anyway? She didn't need someone like that. So, she didn't have a lot of boys calling her all the time; what did that matter? She's a late bloomer. So was I. A lot of girls are late bloomers, but they don't settle for a boy with a face like that, a boy who looks like the devil himself. Whatever happened to Helen, that boy was in on it. I know it. A mother can feel those things."

"I can't believe that," I said. "You can't judge a person by his looks. Just because his face was burned —"

"Looks can warp a person," Mrs. Tuttle continued. "A person has Fate turn on him like that Jeff did, and he gets bitter. He can't have what he once had, and he takes it out on others. I don't have any proof, of course, but I swear, from the first moment that boy walked into our house, I knew he was bad news. I said to Helen afterward, 'You'd better watch out for that one.' She just laughed. She wouldn't listen. And now look what's happened."

She was crying now, the harsh, ragged sobs cutting through the room in jagged little bursts. She raised her large, freckled hands to cover her face, and all I could think was that they might have been Helen's hands except for the heavy gold wedding band on one of the fingers.

There was nothing more that I could bring myself to say.

Mother must have felt the same way, for she simply said, "We'll pray. Please, do call us."

"I will," Mr. Tuttle told us, but his full attention was on his wife.

Outside in the corridor, Mother turned and put her arms around me in a fierce embrace.

"Dear God, Laurie," she said in a strangled voice, "what if it had been you? How could Dad and I have borne it?"

"She is going to live, isn't she?" I asked shakily. It was a stupid question, for, of course, Mother knew no more about the situation than I did, but childhood conditioning is not shaken easily. If Mother said, "Yes," I knew I would feel secure.

But she said, "I hope so," and tightened her arms in a convulsive hug. Then, as quickly as she had reached for me, she released me. We continued down the hall together, not touching, not speaking, yet closer somehow than we had been for many months.

Jeff was still embedded in the chair across from the elevators. His eyes were closed, but they snapped open at our approach.

"Did you learn anything?" he asked us.

"Nothing you probably don't know already," I said.

"The Tuttles" — his voice cracked a little — "they hate me for this, don't they?"

"They're too upset to think reasonably." I know my mother's face in all its variety of expressions. At this moment, there was something in it that I was used to seeing only when she looked at Neal. "Come along, Jeff," she said quietly. "There's no use waiting here. We can't see Helen, and there's no way we can help her."

"I've got to stay," Jeff said gruffly. "I'm responsible. If I hadn't sent her home alone —"

"You couldn't possibly have anticipated this," Mother said. "You did what you thought was the right thing at the time."

"It seemed so practical," Jeff said. "I mean, the show lasted longer than we thought it would, and the last ferry was leaving. If I'd seen her home I'd have missed it. It was late, but I thought she'd be fine in a cab."

"You didn't have a fight, then?" I asked.

"Hell, no! It was just that time got away from us. There was a store Helen wanted to look in, and that threw us late for the show, and everything went later than we'd planned. If I'd missed that boat, what would I have done, slept over at the Tuttles'? That would have gone over like a lead balloon. Mrs. T's had it in for me since the first time she got a look at my face."

"Oh, honey, it's not that," Mother said. It was the first

time I'd heard her use that endearment for anyone but family. "She's a mother hen with one chick, that's all." She put a hand on his arm. "Come, now. We'll all three go back together. There's nothing to be gained by staying. I honestly think the Tuttles are better off without us. They have each other, and that's all they need right now."

Somehow, I've never quite understood how, she got Jeff onto his feet and into the elevator. She kept her hand on his arm all the way to the street as though she were afraid that if she let go he would rush back. There were no available cabs, so we took the bus to the pier, wedged in among holiday shoppers with their armloads of parcels.

The mood on the bus was one of gaiety. People laughed and jostled each other good-naturedly. The woman behind me was humming "Jingle Bells." In front of me a little boy was asking questions in a shrill, piping voice: "Was that man in the store really Santa? Is he the same Santa who comes to our house?"

I stood, holding onto the ceiling strap for support as the bus lurched along with its load of happy passengers, feeling as alien as one of Dad's visitors from outer space. The last time I had been lighthearted seemed a million years ago.

At the landing we found we had just missed the ferry and had over an hour to wait for the next one. Most of that time we sat in silence. I don't know what Jeff and Mother may have been thinking, but in my own mind I was reliving the months since September when a gawky, redhaired girl had offered me lunch money. Had I paid it back? I couldn't remember. I could not even recall how much it had been. Had I given her anything in return for her other gifts — her friendship, her understanding, her tireless willingness to share my problems? "Helen's best friend," Mr. Tuttle had called me. He had been mistaken. Helen had been a friend to me, but I had not been much of one to her.

What had happened last night? There were so many unanswered questions and so few facts to tie them to. Helen had been to the movies. She had returned home in a taxi. She had gotten out, or so we could assume, and paid the driver — and then what? The park was kitty-cornered to the town house. Why would she have crossed the street to go there? It had been cold, and a wind had been blowing. There had been no moon. Why cross to the park and run down a path in absolute darkness?

What had Helen been doing there? Would she ever be able to tell me?

Of course, I assured myself. Of course she will.

But I was not sure that I believed it.

On the ferry Jeff fell asleep. He slid sideways on the seat, and his head came to rest against my shoulder. When we landed he came abruptly awake, jerking up straight, embarrassed.

"Sorry," he muttered.

"That's okay," I said. "You must be exhausted."

"Why don't you come home with us for supper?" Mother asked him.

"No, thanks," Jeff said. "My dad'll be wondering what's happened. Besides, I don't feel hungry." He paused and then added, "Thanks, anyway."

"You're welcome anytime," Mother told him.

We went back to Cliff House, and Mother made dinner. I sat at the table, listening to the chatter of the children and shoving food around my plate with a fork. I glanced across at the spot between Neal and Dad where Helen had once sat and tried to picture her there. "I enjoyed it," she had told me later. "I'm an only child, and things can get pretty dull around our place." Why hadn't I invited her back? As soon as she's well, I will, I told myself. I'll have her out to the island every weekend if she wants to come.

Loneliness swept upon me. Here among the people I loved most, there was someone else I needed.

I lay in bed that night and waited for Lia. I called to her silently, "Come — please, come!" But the room remained empty, and the only sound was the crash of the surf against the rocks.

Finally, I must have dozed off, because I never actually saw her, but at some point during the night I had a dream.

Lia was in it.

"I am here," she told me. "I will always be here. Hold fast to me, Laurie. I am your only friend now."

From then on I slept more peacefully, and when I awoke, the previous day with its painful happenings had become fogged, like a film over which an oily thumb has been drawn, leaving the picture smudged, distorted and unreal.

CHAPTER 11

DECEMBER MOVED FORWARD, LEADING, AS it inevitably does, to Christmas.

Christmas is an absolute. There is no displacing it. No matter what may have occurred during the year, no matter what changes have taken place, Christmas stands at the end of it like the final punctuation after a long and rambling sentence.

"It is over," Christmas tells us. "It is time now to take a deep breath, discard the past, and start again."

I have always loved Christmas, every part of it, the sight, the sound, the smell. This year, however, I could not get a grip on it. Carols slid past my ears, unheard. Tinsel glittered, unappreciated. The traditional spruce imported by boat from the mainland and decorated by the children with familiar handmade ornaments, looked out of place in our living room.

"Take me shopping?" Megan begged me. It was our special ritual, established since her first year in kindergarten.

"Not this year," I started to respond, and then, seeing the bright expectation on her face, I could not disappoint her. We went into the city after school one afternoon and poked through the department stores while Meg made her selections.

"Everything's so beautiful, I just can't decide," she kept saying.

I made my own purchases quickly and with little sense of pleasure — matching shirts for my parents, a game for Neal, a gray stuffed seal for Megan's animal collection, paid for surreptitiously while her back was turned and shoved hurriedly to the bottom of a shopping bag. I saw an emerald green scarf that would have been perfect for Helen, but I did not buy it. I stood looking at it for a long time before deciding not to.

"It's pretty," Meg commented, and I said, "Yes," and turned away. I could not bring myself to confront God with a deadline — "Get her well by Christmas, Lord." It was better to leave things open-ended. "Get her better, Lord, please, in Your own good time. I'm not going to pressure You. Your will be done."

Each day either Mother or I would call the hospital. There was no new information. Helen's vital signs continued to be "stable." She remained unconscious and in Intensive Care.

The day before school let out for the holidays, I was called to the office to find Mr. Tuttle there waiting. He was holding a small box wrapped in silver paper.

"Helen's mother was going through her things," he told me. "She found this with your name on it."

"Oh — please — no!" It was like having somebody slam me hard in the stomach. All the breath went out of me. "I can't take a present. Not now. Not with things the way they are."

"She meant for you to have this, or she wouldn't have bought it." Mr. Tuttle thrust the package into my hand. His face looked tired, and there were lines at the corners of his eyes and mouth that I could not recall having seen there before. "That's Helen for you. She always did do things early. I never knew her to be late, did you?"

"No," I said. "No." I was shaken by his use of the past tense.

"I stopped by the school because I wanted to be sure you got this," Mr. Tuttle said. "I also wanted to say good-bye. We're having Helen transferred to Duke University Hospital in North Carolina. There are doctors there who specialize in head injuries."

"You're taking her away?" It had never occurred to me that Helen might be removed from the vicinity. "You'll be back, though, won't you? As soon as she's better?"

"I think that's unlikely," Mr. Tuttle said.

"But you have a job here and a home!"

"We rent the town house, and one teaching position is pretty much like another." He shook his head. "We moved here because we thought it would be good for Helen. We were wrong."

"Then you'll be moving back out west?"

"I can't say now. The first thing is to get Helen the best care we can. We'll get an apartment near the hospital and see how things go. The school here has released me from my contract, and Mrs. Tuttle and I can both substitute until we're in a position to make further plans."

I regarded him helplessly. "Will you write me how Helen's doing?"

"If there's something definite to report."

"Do you have my address?"

I could tell by his expression that he didn't.

"I'm not thinking too clearly these days," he said apologetically. "Everything's happened so fast."

I tore a page from my notebook and wrote down the address and also our phone number. Mr. Tuttle folded the paper and stuck it in his pocket, and I could not help but wonder if he would ever think of it again.

"You have a nice Christmas," he said. "Give my best to your mother. She's a nice woman. I'm sorry we never had the chance to get to know each other."

We said good-bye, and I put the package in my purse and went back to class. At home that evening I transferred it to the closet shelf where I was storing the gifts I had purchased for the family. I could not bring myself to open it. It was strangely comforting, though, to know that it was there, a final link between Helen and myself.

At dinner that night the children were overflowing with holiday excitement. There had been school parties that afternoon, and both were so full of sweets that they were more ready to talk than to eat. Mother was half with us. She had been commissioned by Natalie Coleson's father to paint a seascape for him to give his wife for Christmas and she had been working on it since early morning and was still too caught up to be able to focus on dinner-table conversation.

As often happens with my parents, their moods balanced. Dad had reached a plateau with his new book and was ready to think about other things. He was expounding on his childhood Christmases, starting with the first he could remember, and had worked his way up to his twelfth ("when I got a book of short stories by Ray Bradbury") when the doorbell rang.

Neal went down to answer it. When he came back he looked puzzled.

"It's Jeff Rankin," he said. "He wants to talk to Laurie."

"For heaven's sake, invite him up," said Mother, coming out of her fog.

"I did," Neal told her. "He said he'd rather wait."

"I'll go down," I said. "I was through eating anyway." I did not have any great desire to relive my father's next thirty Christmases.

Jeff was standing in the entrance hall, looking so surly that I almost turned and went upstairs again. He was leaning against the wall with his hands crammed into the pockets of his parka. His jaw was set, and his eyes held that dark, angry look that meant that he was ready to slash out at somebody.

His greeting was a question.

"Why didn't you tell me they were moving Helen?"

"I didn't know it until today," I said. "It seems like you must have found out the same time I did."

"Who told you? Mrs. T?"

"No, it was Helen's father. He came by school at noon. Helen had gotten me a Christmas present back before the accident. Mr. Tuttle brought it over to give to me, and he told me then." I resented the accusation in his voice. "I would have told you this afternoon if I'd seen you, but you weren't on the ferry."

"I had to stay late for a makeup test."

"Then what are you mad about? How could you expect me to tell you when you weren't there to tell?"

"I thought maybe you'd known about it before." The

fury seemed suddenly to go out of him. "Okay, I'm sorry. I shouldn't have come over. It was just — just —"

"Just what?" I asked more gently.

"Just that I never expected them to take her off this way. I never even got to say good-bye."

"I know." I paused, trying to think what to say next. "Do you want to come upstairs for a while? We're finished eating. Dad's in one of his storytelling moods tonight."

"No thanks." But he made no move to leave.

There was something more wrong here than just his discovery of Helen's transfer. I could not pinpoint what it was, but I could feel the vibrations of some concentrated emotion.

"Let's walk outside," I suggested.

"It's cold."

"Of course it's cold. We don't have to stay long."

I didn't wait for him to answer, but went to the closet and got out my jacket and put it on. When I turned back he was still standing in the same position. The scars on the right side of his face were mottled and ugly under the glare of the overhead light. I remembered how he had looked the first time I had seen him gunning his motorcycle down Beach Road. One of the summertime girls had been seated behind him, squealing in excitement, with her arms clasped tightly around his waist. He had glanced back at her, laughing, shouting something I could not hear over the roar of the engine.

I wondered how long it had been since the last time he had laughed.

"You'd better tell your folks where you're going," he said gruffly. "They'll want to know to come looking if you don't come back."

"Why wouldn't I come back?" I asked.

"Your friend Helen didn't." He opened the door as though offering me a dare.

"You're being ridiculous." I stepped out past him into the night.

Jeff followed me out and pulled the door shut. We stood without speaking while our eyes became adjusted to the dark. Gradually the world began to grow lighter, and I realized that there was a moon, a thin sliver of one, slicing through the edge of a cloud. The air was clean and cold, and the night was still.

"There wasn't any moon for Helen," Jeff said, echoing my thoughts. "It must have been dark as pitch in that park. Why the hell would she have gone there?"

"I don't know," I said. "Nobody does."

"Her mother's figured it out, or thinks she has."

He began to walk, and I fell into step beside him. The path along the side of Cliff House was so familiar that my feet knew it by heart. It was Jeff who stumbled, and I took his arm to steady him.

"What do you mean?" I asked.

"She phoned me this evening. That's how I learned about Helen. She said they were getting her out of here, away to a 'safe place' where I couldn't get at her."

"Mrs. Tuttle said that!" I exclaimed. "But it's not true at all! They're taking Helen to Duke because there are specialists there who can help her. Mr. Tuttle told me that himself."

"Mrs. T thinks I did it," Jeff continued. "She thinks I was with Helen in the park."

"She can't believe that," I said, outraged. "The cab driver must have a record of the trips he made that night. He knows whether he carried one passenger or two, and if the facts he gave hadn't fit with your story, the police would have followed up on it."

"She said she warned Helen about me. She said the moment she saw me she knew I was going to be bad news. 'But I couldn't stop her,' she said. 'Helen was sorry for you. She was trying to be kind, and then you attacked her.' "

"Oh, Jeff!" I tightened my hold on his arm, aching for him, wishing that somehow I could absorb the pain. "She didn't mean that. She was just yelling things into the wind. Helen didn't go out with you for any reason except that she liked you."

"I shouldn't have let her go home alone."

"It made sense. You had no way of knowing she wouldn't go straight into the house."

We had reached the end of the path. Cliff House stood solidly behind us, a great, dark hulk, and before us lay the rocks and beyond them the sea. The moon kept playing at the cloud's edge, sending sparkles of silver to reflect in the pools in the rock hollows, and the sea made a sighing sound as it moved rhythmically in and out of the mermaids' caves.

"You don't go out there anymore, do you?" Jeff asked suddenly.

"Out on those rocks?" I was disconcerted by the abrupt change of subject. "I never have. I told you that."

"Don't give me that, Laurie. I saw you there myself."

"No, you didn't," I insisted. "Really."

"I know what I saw," Jeff said. "I know what you look like by this time. You were either there in person or using astral projection."

"What?" I was so startled that I dropped his arm and stepped back to stare at him. The moonlight came from behind him, and I could not make out his expression. "Why did you say that? What do you know about projection?"

"Nothing personally." He seemed surprised by my reaction. "Helen used to talk about it sometimes, that's all."

"What did she say?" I demanded. "What did she tell you? Why would Helen have discussed something like that with you?"

"Hey, calm down, will you?" Jeff said. "I didn't mean anything. I was just talking to be talking. It's an interest of Helen's, not mine. I don't even think I believe in it."

"Something had to make you bring it up!"

"I was reading about it today, and the word stuck in my mind. Helen picked up some books on the subject the night she had her accident. I ran out of things to read and started leafing through one of them."

"She bought them the night of the accident?"

"That's what threw us late," Jeff said. "We were headed for the show when we passed this secondhand store with books in the window. Helen wanted to go in and look. She said she had a friend who was into that sort of thing. She bought a couple, and by the time we got to the movie the feature was half over, so we stayed for the next. I was carrying the books, and with all the confusion finding a cab and everything, I forgot to hand them to her." He paused. Then realization dawned. "Oh, I get it now. You must be the 'friend.' Do you want me to bring them over?"

"When you're through with them. I can wait if you're in the middle of reading them." My attempt at nonchalance came too late. After my previous reaction it sounded absurd. At least, though, we were past the subject of Helen's injury and Mrs. Tuttle's phone call.

"I was just skimming it," Jeff said. "I hadn't planned on reading all of it. Maybe now I will, though." There was a moment's silence. Then he said slowly, "You did go onto those rocks one evening, didn't you? It was about a month ago around dusk."

"No," I told him. "I didn't."

"I wasn't serious when I asked you that about projecting. It was just meant as a joke."

"I know that."

"I did see you. Or, I thought I did."

"I'm sure you did think that," I said. "Look, Jeff, there's no sense in our discussing this. You don't believe in astral projection, and I don't blame you. I couldn't accept it myself until just recently." A question occurred to me. "What were you doing here the night you thought you saw me? There's no reason for anyone to come out this way unless he's coming to Cliff House."

"I walk here sometimes because you live here," Jeff said.

It was not an answer I expected.

We did not talk as we walked back toward Cliff House, but halfway there his hand found mine and closed around it. It was a warm, strong hand, and I felt no desire to draw my own away.

When Lia came that night there was something different about her, something stronger and more intense. She was not the same person who had lingered at my bedside on previous nights to give me reassurance through the turmoil of my dreams.

"It is time," she said.

"Now? Tonight?" Of course, I planned to learn to

project. Somehow, though, I had taken for granted the fact that I would be the one to say when.

The decision was suddenly not mine to make.

"It's simple," Lia assured me. "You have the ability. You are from a people who have a heritage of spiritual power. Our mother could travel anywhere she willed herself. She learned in early childhood. I taught myself to project when I was seven. If we who share your blood can travel in this manner, you should be able to."

"I'll try." There had been a time when I had almost done it. The night I had slept at Helen's and had focused home upon Cliff House. Had that been projection, or a form of dreaming?

"Before you start," Lia told me, "you must concentrate upon your destination."

This I knew at once. I would go to Helen.

"Cast your soul into space," Lia directed. "Lift away from your body. It is a sudden thing. A leap. You must disconnect from the physical and spring to the astral plane."

How easy she made it sound! I knotted the muscles of my mind, and, with all my mental strength, I shoved upward.

I will myself — to go — to Helen!

For an instant I thought I had accomplished it. Then, with a rush of disappointment, I became aware of the weight of the blankets upon my body and realized that I was in exactly the same position that I had been before.

"It didn't work," I said to Lia.

"Were you thinking in words?"

"Well, yes. I suppose I was. How else does one think?"

"Erase them," Lia told me. "Words nail you to the earth. You must lift, not with your mind but with your soul."

I tried to do this. I pictured Helen, flat and far in a hospital bed. Her head was bandaged.

Helen — I'm with you — Helen!

With that, I was into words again, and back at Cliff House. Helen was far away.

Helen! The very name was a word.

"Erase them!"

"I can't think without words," I protested.

"You can," Lia said. "What if you had been born deaf and had never heard a human voice? You would still be able to think, wouldn't you? It is a different kind of thought. Pure. Free of restraints. Just lift — and go!"

"I'm trying." Despite myself, my mind insisted on articulating. *I am in the hospital. I am entering the room. I am with my friend.*

"Erase the words!"

"I can't!"

But I continued to try until my mind became numb with exhaustion, and I could think no more.

CHAPTER 12

I TRIED AGAIN THE FOLLOWING NIGHT, and the night after that. Each time the results were the same. I began to feel as battered as though I had been hurling myself time after time against a concrete wall. As my frustration mounted, I became irritated, not only with myself, but with Lia.

"Why can't I do it? You made it sound so easy!"

"Before you can move, you must detach from the physical."

"But how?"

"Let go! Release your hold on the earth! Let go of the words that are tying you down!"

There was something in her voice that was near to anger. Why was that, I wondered. What was it to Lia if I did or did not learn to do this? She herself could leave her own body at will. She was free to travel where she wished. Why should it matter so much to her that I be able to also?

Lying on my bed with my eyes squeezed shut, I could feel the vibrations of her anger reaching to engulf me. They rolled over me like icy waves, and I shivered, unable to comprehend what lay behind them.

"Try again, Laurie," Lia urged. "Try again."

"I am trying!"

I no longer knew if it was myself or my sister whom I was trying to please. With all my strength I concentrated upon willing myself across the miles. I could see a building like a hospital, and in my mind, I moved toward it. I entered through the front door and was in the lobby. Somewhere close by in one of the rooms off a corridor on a floor above, my friend was lying.

Helen! The name flashed into my mind, and I was in my bed again.

"I'm back," I whispered.

"Back!" Lia was contemptuous. "You never left. To think about a place is not the same as putting yourself there. If you really wanted to —"

"I do want to!" For some reason I was beginning to feel frightened. I wished that Lia would not be so insistent. I had liked her better the way she had been before, gentle and supportive.

"If you want to, *then do it!*" The command seemed to fill the room.

"I'm tired."

"Tired or not, you must keep trying. It is the only way!"

And so I tried, and failed again. This time I knew that I would fail, for I had no remaining energy. Lia must at last have realized this, for she withdrew. She did not tell me that she was leaving, but I felt her presence evaporate, and a sense of peace came upon me. My tension vanished, and I slept.

The next day was the twenty-fourth of December. Our tree had been up and decorated for over a week, but Neal and Megan were still finding new things to hang upon it.

Meg spent the morning fashioning a long looping chain of red and gold construction paper to twine around the overloaded limbs, and Neal sat at the kitchen table, gilding the largest member of his starfish collection to be the Star of Wonder. Dad closed down his typewriter and honored the occasion by making cookies, something he does every now and then because he has a sweet tooth. Mother, who had completed the oil for Natalie's parents the day before, devoted her morning to helping Mr. Coleson select a frame.

I wrapped my gifts for the family (Meg had wrapped hers the instant we got home from our shopping expedition) and was placing them under the tree with the others when Mr. Coleson came down the stairs from Mother's studio and paused at the doorway to the living room.

"How do you like it?" he asked, displaying his purchase as proudly as though he had painted it himself. "Your mother thought the natural wood would be most effective, and after trying it with some of the more ornate frames, I came to think she was right."

"It's lovely," I agreed appreciatively.

The frame they had chosen was a weathered gray with the deeply grained look of driftwood. The sea in the painting was also of varied tones of gray dotted with whitecaps, and in the foreground a child in a yellow T-shirt, looking from the back very much like Neal, leaned against a porch railing that might have been constructed from the same wood as the frame.

"I think so too." Mr. Coleson beamed down at the picture possessively. Then, in a friendly manner, he asked, "How have you been, Laurie? We haven't been seeing much of you lately. You're coming to Natalie's caroling party tonight, aren't you?"

"Why — no — I don't think I'll be able to make it," I said awkwardly. "In our family we usually stay home on Christmas Eve."

"That's refreshing," Mr. Coleson said. "Sometimes I wish Nat weren't quite so social. It's party, party, party all through the holidays. That's how young people are, I guess, but it seems sometimes to be almost too much of a good thing."

"I like parties," volunteered Megan, who was sitting on the floor in front of the fireplace, gluing her chain together. "I'd go to one any night I got asked."

"That's how Natalie feels," Mr. Coleson said good-naturedly. "Well, Merry Christmas, girls!"

"Merry Christmas," Meg and I responded with different degrees of enthusiasm.

After Mr. Coleson had continued on down the stairs to take the painting to his car, Meg turned to me in bewilderment.

"Why aren't you going? I bet Dad and Mother would let you. I heard them just the other day talking about how you never go anywhere anymore."

"I'm not going," I said, "for the simple reason that I wasn't invited."

"Then why didn't you say that?"

"Mr. Coleson was trying to be friendly," I told her. "I didn't want to embarrass him."

"Did you not get asked because you and Gordon broke up?"

"I imagine that's it," I said. "I got accepted by that crowd because I started going with him, and now I guess I'm out of it again. Don't worry about it, Meg. It doesn't bother me. I've got other things on my mind these days."

"It would bother *me*," Megan said. "Nat Coleson is just plain stinky. If I were you I'd call her and tell her that if she's going to act like that —"

Her sage advice was interrupted by the ring of the telephone.

Meg dropped her paper chain next to the glue bottle and scrambled hastily to her feet.

"I bet that's her right now, calling to invite you! Maybe she just couldn't get you before."

"I wouldn't stake my life on it if I were you," I said wryly.

The phone stopped ringing abruptly as Dad picked up the extension in the kitchen. A moment later his voice rang up the stairwell. "Laurie? It's for you!"

"See? I told you!" Meg exclaimed with satisfaction.

"I still don't believe it." I crossed to the wall phone and picked up the receiver. "Hello?"

"Laurie?" The male voice took me by surprise. For one instant I thought it was Gordon. Perhaps Joyce had fallen through on him, and with a party tonight and no date, he was going to try to pick up the pieces of our old relationship.

Then the voice said, "I've got those books for you," and I realized it was Jeff.

"Did you read them?" I asked him.

"Yeah. They're weird. At first the whole thing sounded crazy, and then I hit this part about tests they've been running at places like the Stanford Research Center. There was this guy named Swann. Have you heard about him?"

"No," I said.

"The scientists at the Center did a lot of experiments using him for a subject. For one of them they'd have him lie down, and there would be a platform suspended over him up near the ceiling. There were a lot of different objects on it, and a side railing sticking up so they couldn't be seen from below. Swann would project himself up there. His body would stay on the bed, but the 'second self' — that's what the author called it — would float up to the platform and look over the rail. Then it would return to the body, and Swann would sit up and draw pictures of the stuff up there."

"Did it say how he did it?" I asked.

"There wasn't a set of rules, but it talked about this special sort of energy he uses. When he's out of his body he looks like he's asleep, but the scientists could tell the difference by measuring his brain-wave patterns."

"I want to read about it," I said eagerly. "Can I come over and get them?"

"I was thinking —" He paused.

"What?"

"What I was going to say was maybe I could bring them over tonight. Except I just remembered, it's Christmas Eve. I guess you probably have something planned."

"No," I said. "I'll just be here with the family."

"Well, maybe I'll stop over then. There's nothing going on at my place. My dad's got a date on the mainland with this woman he's going with."

"Why don't you have dinner with us, then?" I asked him.

"On Christmas Eve? Your folks wouldn't want an outsider."

"They'll be glad to have you," I said, hoping this was true. "Mother invited you over before, remember?"

"Well, I don't know —"

"You're going to be coming anyway to bring the books. You might as well eat while you're here."

"It's not like I'm going to starve," Jeff said, trying to make a joke of the situation. "There's plenty of stuff in our refrigerator, and I'm used to cooking for myself."

"Then come early and make the gravy," I told him. "That's something nobody here is good at. We'll see you around five-thirty, okay?"

"Well, okay. Thanks."

I hung up the receiver and went down to the kitchen to tell my parents to expect a dinner guest. The place smelled great. Dad had two plates of sugar cookies cooling on the counter and was in the process of putting another batch into the oven. Neal had his golden starfish drying on a piece of newspaper, and, flushed with this initial success, was busy gilding a conch shell. Mother was relaxing in a chair, doing nothing, looking happy and limp the way she does when one painting project is completed and she hasn't yet started on another.

"That was Jeff on the phone," I said. "I invited him for dinner. I hope that's okay."

"Is this the guy who came over the other night and wouldn't come upstairs?" Dad asked, frowning. "Who is he, anyway? This is a special night, you know."

"It's the Rankin boy, Jim," Mother said. "You remember the one who got burned so badly a couple of years ago?"

"Pete Rankin's kid? Sure, I know who he is. I've seen him in the village." He turned to me. "Is he a particular friend of yours, Laurie?"

"Yes," I said, surprising myself with the firmness of my reply. "His father isn't going to be home tonight, and I thought —"

"Of course," Mother said. "Jeff's a nice boy. I'm glad you thought to ask him. What time did you invite him for?"

"I told him five-thirty," I said. "But that doesn't mean we need to eat then. He does the cooking at his place, so we can put him to work in the kitchen."

"Those bachelor pads!" Dad exclaimed. "How do such men survive? Why, if your mother weren't here to burn dinner for us every night —"

"Now, Jim, stop that," Mother countered. "I haven't burned a meal in ages."

"Of course not. You've been serving sandwiches."

"You know I had to get that painting finished!" And they were off and running, squabbling along in the way they do when they are both feeling on top of things. Neal looked up from his artwork and grinned. I winked at him, feeling happier suddenly than I had in a long time. On the way out of the room I stole a couple of cookies.

I went up the stairs, glancing in at Megan, who was up on a chair, redecorating the Christmas tree, and continued on to my bedroom. The first thing I noticed when I entered was the light. It was funny light, slanting in through the glass doors and bouncing back and forth off the walls with a dizzying effect. I stopped and blinked. My eyes felt strange as though my pupils were expanding and contracting in rapid succession. I blinked again, closed the door, and went over to the bed.

I sat down on the end of it and found myself gazing up at Lia.

She was there, standing over me. In broad daylight. In early afternoon. She was there, not as a shadow, not as Megan's "ghosty," but real. Solid-looking. Less than a foot away.

"Why did you ask that boy over?" she demanded.

I stared at her, stunned by the fact that she was here in this absolute form. I almost felt that I could reach out and touch her.

"Because I wanted him here," I said.

"Why?"

"Because — well, he has the books —"

"He is not to come!" Her eyes were blazing, those almond-shaped eyes so much like mine, yet now so radically different. I knew my eyes could never look like that. I knew I would not want them to. The fury in her voice was an extension of the anger I had heard there before, but it was greatly intensified.

I felt a flash of fear, but I kept my voice steady.

"I like Jeff. I'll see as much of him as I choose."

"He does not belong in your life!"

"He does if I want him there," I said defiantly. This was a different sort of confrontation from any we had had before. There was no shield of darkness to separate us. I would not be intimidated.

"Who are you to tell me who belongs in my life and who doesn't?"

"I am your *twin sister!*" Lia hurled the words at me as though they explained everything.

"So what if you are? That doesn't give you the right to run my life! You can't tell me what to do! You can't choose my friends for me!"

"Oh, can't I?" She let the question hang there a moment between us and then asked more gently, "Just who are your friends, sister Laurie?"

"My friends are — why, they're — they're —" I could not give an answer.

"Gordon? Natalie? Darlene?" She enunciated the names with exaggerated care. "You used to consider those people friends, didn't you?"

"Yes — but —"

"Blane? Tommy? Mary Beth?" she was laughing at me. *"Helen?"*

"What have you done?" I whispered in horror. "What in God's name have you *done?"*

"If you care anything about this Jeff, you had better phone him now," Lia said. "Tell him not to come. Tell him never to come here again. If you don't, you will carry guilt upon your shoulders for the rest of your days."

"Get out of my room," I said shakily. "Get out now! Go back to wherever it is you come from!" Helen had been right; Lia was evil! Helen had recognized this, even when I had insisted otherwise.

"You're alone," Lia said quietly. "You have no friends — not any longer. Your parents are not really your parents. The children you think of as your brother and sister are no more to you than any other youngsters you might pick out on a school playground. Our real mother is dead. Our real father deserted us before we were born. I am all you have, Laurie. All you have."

"Go!" I told her. "Go! Get out of here!" My voice went out of control. It rose with a shriek. "Go, and don't come back!"

"Laurie?" My mother's voice called from the far side of my door. "Laurie, what's the matter?" She didn't wait for me to answer but threw it open and stood there, framed in the doorway.

I stared at her as though seeing her for the first time. The pale, freckled skin. The sky blue eyes. The fine, light hair, beginning at the sides to soften into silver. She and Dad, Neal and Megan, were a unit in themselves. They were the Strattons. And I — who was I?

There was one thing I was sure of. I was not like Lia! I might look like her, but there the resemblance ended.

And for the first time, there was someone who could see us together!

"Mother, look!" I cried. "Now you know what's been happening!"

But even as I spoke, Lia was gone. I was pointing at nothing. The room was empty. Everything was as it should have been, except for the bouncing patterns of the afternoon light.

"It is odd, isn't it?" Mother said, thinking this was what I meant. "I've never seen light quite like this. I was going up to the studio to study it a bit, to see whether there was some way I could use it in a painting. Then I thought I heard you call out. Is everything okay?"

"Yes," I said quickly. "Fine. It wasn't anything."

"Are you sure?" She was looking at me oddly. "You look tired. Your eyes are funny."

"I haven't been sleeping well lately." That was true enough.

"You're worried about Helen," Mother said with an understanding nod. "It's terrible to have a situation hang on like this. Perhaps there will be good news soon. That's what Christmas is all about, isn't it? Good news? We can hope."

"I'm hoping," I said. "All the time."

"Why don't you stretch out and take a nap? You'll want to feel rested for tonight. And for tomorrow. You know what happens when the kids hit the Christmas stockings."

"Yes," I said, trying to smile. "It's a wild day."

After she left the room I did lie down on the bed and shut my eyes. I didn't mean to sleep, but when I opened them the odd, sparkling light was gone and the room had settled into shadows.

It's past five-thirty, I thought, struggling to drag myself back to consciousness. Jeff is probably already here. I should have been down there to greet him. It's awful to leave somebody who's never been here before to try to make conversation with the family.

But when I put on a fresh blouse and combed my hair and went downstairs, I found that I need not have worried. Jeff had not arrived.

At six-fifteen I phoned his home. There was no answer.

"He must be on his way," I said to Mother.

"That's all right," she said. "I didn't plan for us to eat much before six-thirty anyway."

At six-forty-five, when Jeff still had not come, I called again and listened to the repeated sound of the phone shrilling unanswered through an empty house.

At seven-ten we sat down to dinner.

"Is this what being 'stood up' means?" Meg asked with interest.

CHAPTER 13

CHRISTMAS DAY BEGAN EARLY FOR US AS it must for every family in a home where there are children. Neal and Megan were in my room at dawn, bouncing onto my bed and jerking me into consciousness with shrieks of excitement.

"Santa's come!" Meg squealed. "The stockings are lumpy!"

Neal, from the mature vantage point of his eleven years, said condescendingly, "She peeked already," and then added with honesty, "So did I. That pile of stuff under the tree got higher since last night."

At their ages there was no way in the world that either of them could still have been a true believer, but the game was not to admit it. "When people stop believing in him, Santa stops coming," Dad had always told us. "That's when they stop having stockings." Faced with this ultimatum, I myself had professed absolute belief until I was almost into my teens.

Even now the anticipation and the sense of wonder continued. There was still something magical about rising on Christmas morning to find that sometime while I had been sleeping *he* had come.

This morning, however, it was different. I felt tired and uncaring. The pale gray of the sky outside the balcony doors made me want to roll over and press my face into my pillow.

"The sun's not even up yet," I snapped at the children. "Why don't you go back to bed for a while? The presents will still be there an hour from now."

"But it's *Christmas!*" Neal exclaimed. "Dad and Mother are getting up. They said to come wake you."

The astonishment in his voice made me feel guilty for my Scrooge-like behavior.

"Okay," I said more gently. "Run on down and get started. I'll be along in a minute, as soon as I can get myself into gear."

They went rushing off like racers hearing the starting gun, and I sank back onto the pillow, fighting the desire to haul the covers up over my head and bury myself again beneath protective layers of sleep.

But I couldn't. I was awake now. The day must be faced, and with it the ego-shattering reality of the fact that, as Meg had so bluntly put it, I had been "stood up." It was something that had never happened to me before. Whatever Gordon's faults may have been, he, at least, had been reliable. If he and I made a date to do something, we did it.

"That Rankin kid needs a lesson in manners," Dad had remarked last night as he attempted to force a carving knife through a loin of pork that had shriveled into a dried-out lump. "If he wasn't coming, he could at least have let us know, so we could have eaten while the food was still chewable."

"Maybe he didn't understand Laurie was asking him for

tonight," Mother said. "He might have thought she meant tomorrow."

"He understood perfectly," I told them. "Some emergency must have come up. He'll call and explain it, I'm sure."

But the evening had passed, and the phone had not rung. We finished dinner and sang some carols and read through the Christmas story, which was our holiday custom. The kids hung up their stockings and were sent to bed, and Mother decided she was sleepy too, and Dad said he thought he would forgo his evening writing stint and turn in early also to fuel himself for the morning.

"I think I'll try calling Jeff again," I said.

Dad regarded me with disapproval. "I wouldn't push it, Laurie. He's the one who ought to be doing the calling. If he forgot us, let him do a double-take in the morning and get himself over here with an apology."

"I can't believe he just forgot," I said. "It's not like Jeff had some kind of roaring social life so he couldn't keep track of his invitations. I'll sleep better if I can get in touch with him and find out what happened."

But when I dialed what was getting to be a familiar number, there was still no answer. I let the phone continue ringing for a long time. At last I replaced the receiver on the hook and went up the stairs to my room. It was an empty room. There was no sign of Lia. I changed into my pajamas and got into bed, hesitating a moment before reaching for the light.

Then I thought, what difference does it make? She's gotten strong enough so she can appear in daylight as well as darkness. If she wants to come, she will come, whether the light's on or not.

Defiantly I clicked it off and closed my eyes. Sleep did not come quickly, but when it did I slept heavily, undisturbed by dreams.

And now it was Christmas morning, a time for joyful celebration, and I was not in a mood for it. Overnight my concern for Jeff had turned to anger. No matter what had happened, there was no excuse for his not having called me. I had thought we were friends, but friends didn't treat each other this way.

"Laurie!" Dad called from below. "Get a move on! We can't keep the kids on hold indefinitely!"

"I'm coming!" Resolutely, I shoved the whole thing to the back of my mind and got out of bed. It *was* Christmas, after all, and I might as well try to enjoy it. I put on my robe and went downstairs to a living room that was a-twinkle with tree lights and the children's sparkling eyes.

The stockings took five minutes. The kids tore through them like mad things. Then we had breakfast, another family custom, because it made the suspense last longer. When we did get to the presents under the tree, we took turns opening them in order to prolong the excitement as long as possible. Everybody exclaimed happily over everything, and my own pile of loot rose higher and higher as clothes and books and records accumulated.

The last gift was the present from Helen. I held it gingerly, wondering how a box so light could contain anything at all.

"I don't think I ought to open it," I said softly. "I think I should keep it wrapped and open it later after she's well."

"It's a Christmas present," Mother said. "She meant for you to have it today. I'm sure that's what she would want, honey."

"I guess you're right." Yet, still, I sat with the tiny box

in my hands, reluctant to unwrap it. I had a strange feeling that once this was accomplished, the last remaining link between Helen and myself would be broken.

"Go on, Laurie," Neal urged impatiently. "Let's see what she gave you!"

"I bet it's jewelry," Megan said. "The box is so little."

"Okay, okay. Hold onto your horses, everybody." I untied the ribbon and drew the box out of its encasement of silver paper. Everyone leaned forward to see.

"Toothpicks!" Neal said, reading the label. "That's crazy. Why would Helen give you toothpicks?"

"I'm sure she didn't," Mother said. "She just used the box to put something else in."

The lid was secured with Scotch tape. I slipped my fingernail across it, and the top sprang up, exposing layers of white tissue. I moved them aside with the tip of my finger and caught a flash of blue.

"It's a bird!" exclaimed Megan.

Carefully I lifted the turqouise figure from the box. It was suspended on a thin chain of silver beads.

"A gull?" Neal asked.

"It's an eagle," I told him. I held it out on the palm of my hand so the rest of the family could view it. The wings of the bird were spread wide, and the head was thrust forward as though it were in flight. It seemed to be looking down, examining the earth below.

"That's Indian-made," Dad said. "And it's obviously hand-carved. Look, you can see the outline of each of the wing feathers. Helen couldn't possibly have gotten it here. It must be something she brought with her from the Southwest."

"It is," I said. "A Navajo boy carved it for her. She wore

it all the time. I can't believe she would give it away." My eyes stung. "I don't deserve this. If she were here, I'd make her take it back."

"No, you wouldn't," Mother said. "If Helen gave it to you, it's because she wanted you to have it to wear. The fact that it meant so much to her makes it doubly meaningful. Here, let me help you put it on."

I lifted the chain to my neck, fumbling awkwardly with the tiny clasp. Mother's deft hands took over, and she had just succeeded in getting it fastened when the telephone rang.

Meg was on her feet in a flash.

"That's Kimmie! She promised she'd call as soon as she got her presents opened!" A moment later, however, she was saying, "No, he isn't. No, he hasn't been here. Do you want to talk to my sister?" She turned to me, extending the receiver. "It's Mr. Rankin."

"Jeff's father?" As I took the phone from her hand, I found that my own was shaking. "Hello," I said. "This is Laurie."

"Pete Rankin here," an unfamiliar voice boomed. "I'm trying to track down my wandering son. Do you know where he might be?"

"No," I told him. "I haven't seen or even talked with Jeff since yesterday."

"What time did he leave your place last night?"

"He didn't," I said. "I mean, he was never here."

"That's odd. I thought he was going to be eating dinner with you folks."

"He was," I said, "but he never came. We thought he might have forgotten."

"He didn't do that," Mr. Rankin said. "He was real

pleased about the invitation. It was the last thing he told me as I was leaving."

"Then why didn't he come? And why did he let you think he *did* come?"

Nothing about the situation made sense.

"I haven't seen Jeff since yesterday," Mr. Rankin told me. "I missed the last ferry and stayed over on the mainland with a friend. I tried to give Jeff a call, but I couldn't get an answer."

"And he isn't home now?"

"Doesn't seem to be. I just got here myself ten minutes ago. I don't know where he could have run off to this early. I thought maybe he'd talked to you about his plans."

"I didn't see him last night." I repeated the statement numbly. "I don't know where he is."

"Well, no problem. I'll call around and see if I can find him. He's probably at somebody's house. There was a party or something last night, wasn't there? I heard some kids on the ferry talking about it. Maybe he went to that and wound up going home with somebody."

"The party was at the Colesons'," I said. "I'm sure, though, that Jeff didn't go."

"You never know. He might have stopped off there on his way to your place and gotten roped in somehow. I know how those things can happen. I was a teenager once myself." He didn't sound worried. "If he turns up there, you have him call me, okay? Meanwhile, I'll check with the Colesons."

"Yes," I said. "I'll do that. And if he comes home, please have him call *me*."

The room was strangely silent as I hung up the telephone. Even Megan for once had her mouth closed.

"Jeff is missing," I told them.

"What do you mean?" Dad said. "He's been gone all night?"

"Mr. Rankin isn't sure. He wasn't there himself. He says he just got home, and Jeff isn't there."

"Maybe he got up early and went off someplace," Neal said.

"That's possible," I conceded. "Still, when you add in the fact that he didn't show up here last night, it starts to get scary."

"What was all that about the Colesons?" asked Mother.

"Nat gave a party yesterday. Mr. Rankin is going to check and see if Jeff was there."

"Perhaps he was," Dad said. "Maybe he thought a party would be more fun than sitting around here on a holiday evening. It's a possibility."

"No, it isn't," I said firmly. "It just isn't. Jeff doesn't run with Nat's crowd. He's a loner. He has been ever since his accident. Natalie wouldn't have invited him, and if she had, he wouldn't have accepted."

"Let's take the bikes and ride into the village," Neal suggested. "That way we can check out the road."

"Yes, let's," I said gratefully. The idea of taking action of any kind was better than remaining at home doing nothing.

"I can't think much will be accomplished by that," said Mother. "Jeff was invited for five-thirty when it was still light out. All he had to do was walk Beach Road from the village to Cliff House. I can't believe he could have run into any problem along that strip."

"Look what happened to Helen," I reminded her. "All she had to do was get out of a cab and walk into her house. Crazy things do sometimes happen to people."

"Yes, they do," Mother acknowledged. Then she added softly, "I guess I just don't want to face up to the possibility. It seems as though that boy has had enough trouble in his life without something more happening."

"Laurie will worry less if she's out doing something," Dad said, and Mother nodded.

"Yes, go ahead, dear. Perhaps he *did* have some sort of freak accident on his way over here. At any rate, we'll all feel better if we can rule out that possibility."

So Neal and I rode our bikes into the village, and Mother had been right; the trip served no purpose. Somewhere in the back of my mind I suppose I had a picture of Jeff in the same situation as Helen, lying injured and helpless along the roadside, but there was no sign of him, and there wasn't even any area where an accident might reasonably have occurred. Beach Road was smooth and flat, lined with nothing more threatening than sea oats and beach grass. Any danger spots were along the cliff walks, many yards away. The village, when we reached it, was like a ghost town with the shops closed tight and no one on the streets or sidewalks. Neal and I pedaled home feeling as though we were the only two people in the world.

It was almost noon when we arrived back at Cliff House. We put away the bikes and entered through the back door. The clack of Dad's typewriter told us that he was busy making up for the time he had lost the previous evening. I found myself resenting the fact that he could divide his life up so easily. When he was writing he wasn't worried about anything or anyone except the people in his book.

Mother was in the living room feeding Christmas wrappings into the fireplace. She answered my question before I could ask it.

"No, Mr. Rankin hasn't called back."

"Do you think *I* should call *him?*"

"No, I don't," Mother said. "When there's news, he'll let you know, and until then it's better that his line stays open in case Jeff tries to reach him." There was sympathy in her voice. "There's nothing to do but wait, honey. I know how hard that is. Meg's in the kitchen making lunch. Why don't you and Neal go get something?"

"I'm not hungry," I said.

"Then how about helping me with this clean-up? Like Dad said, it's better if you can keep yourself busy."

So for the next quarter hour I picked up boxes and paper and ribbons and helped Mother burn them. Then I collected the gifts I had received that morning and carried them to my room. On any other such occasion I would have taken this opportunity to examine and enjoy them, but today I merely piled them into the bookcase and bureau. Once this was done, I just stood there, at a loss as to what to do with myself. The long afternoon lay ahead of me, and then the evening. Surely there would be word of Jeff's whereabouts by dinnertime. He had to go home to eat, didn't he? Or, if he didn't, he would phone his father. He had probably gone off somewhere, not even pausing to think that he would be worrying anyone. But —

But where on earth did someone find to go on *Christmas?*

My head was beginning to ache, and the room seemed suddenly to be closing in on me. Impulsively, I slid open the door and stepped out onto the balcony. The cold salt air struck me, full and damp, and I shivered uncontrollably. It seemed a million years ago that I had stood in this same spot with the September sun streaming down upon me, watching the tiny prams dart like rainbow pollywogs across the satin surface of the summer sea.

Today the ocean was gray and empty. Even now at midday the fog lay thick upon it, obscuring the dividing line between the water and sky. I moved to the railing and turned my gaze to the slick, dark rocks below me. "You don't go out there, do you?" Jeff had asked.

Now the question in reverse occurred to me. Was it possible that Jeff might have tried to walk out upon those rocks last night?

Of course not, I told myself. Jeff was no idiot. He was completely aware of the danger. It was *he* who had warned *me*. And what would his motive have been? The shell path from Beach Road led directly past our kitchen door.

But — what if he *did* attempt it, a silent voice screamed within my head. What if for some crazy reason he *did?*

He didn't. He couldn't have.

It was at that moment I saw it, a spot of color where no bright color should have been. A touch of red against the dullness of the black and brown and green, it lay beneath me, a little to the left.

I saw it. And I knew.

I left the balcony, not even taking the time to close the sliding doors, and hurried through my room and down the stairs. Neal and I had left our parkas in the entrance hall. I snatched mine up and was still thrusting my arms into the sleeves as I let myself out into the bleak December afternoon.

Once outside, I broke into a run along the path by the side of the house. It terminated where it met the rocks, and that was where I found them — two books, set carefully one on top of the other.

One had a red cover.

So, Jeff had not forgotten, he had not let me down. He had come as he had said he would — this far and no farther. Then he had set down the books and — gone where?

There could only be one answer. Slowly, I moved across the flat surface of the ledge, my eyes on the drop-off that led to the lower tiers of rock. I knew the spot where Neal had once fallen, and I headed there, bracing myself for what it was that I might find. My legs felt weak, and my mouth was sour with the metallic taste of fear.

The farther I walked, the slicker the rocks became. The moss growth increased, and the water came surging up through the crevices in bursts of froth. I felt icy foam against my ankles, and the crash of the waves was thunder in my ears.

I should go back, I knew, and get Dad to accompany me, but I kept moving forward, drawn to face whatever it was that must be faced as quickly as possible.

I never got there.

Several yards from the edge, a void seemed to gape beneath me. I screamed — I think I screamed — but perhaps I didn't; perhaps the scream was in my head. My only vivid recollection is of that instant in which I seemed to hang motionless in empty air. Then I went plunging down between two widely spaced rocks into the mermaids' caverns below.

CHAPTER 14

THE MERMAIDS' CAVERNS! MEGAN LOVED to talk about them during those moments at bedtime when she wanted to make the evening last a little longer.

"There are giant rooms," she would tell us, "lighted with phosphorus, so everything in them glows green. The walls are made of coral, and all over the place there are jewels from pirate treasures. And there are mirrors on the ceilings so the mermaids can look at themselves when they comb their hair."

"And what do they do down there after they get their hair taken care of?" I asked her once, enjoying the sound of the chirping little voice as she kept the story going.

"They sing a lot," she said, "and — and —" She paused and frowned thoughtfully. "Actually, I don't really know, Laurie. I've never been down there. Maybe someday one of us will get to go."

It's strange how such thoughts can occur to people in moments of trauma, ridiculous thoughts that make no sense at all. Perhaps it is something that happens in the brain to protect your sanity, a sort of diversion to diffuse the horror of a situation until you regain the strength to handle it. I did not lose consciousness. I was aware of everything — of the pain and of the darkness and of the splash of water and the sharp, dank odor of fishy things that had never seen the light. By rights I should have been thinking death, and instead I was thinking mermaids.

Now I will know. I will be able to tell Meg what they do all day.

I closed my eyes to make the darkness seem more natural. I could even believe I was dreaming, especially when a cold hand touched my cheek and the voice of a merman asked softly, "Are you alive?"

I tried to say, "Yes," but to my surprise I found that I could not get the word from my mind into my mouth and out past my lips. Perhaps I *am* dead, I thought. But if so, then I shouldn't be hurting.

Experimentally, I opened my eyes and found that I was not in unrelieved blackness after all. There was a faint light coming from somewhere. With effort, I turned my head and found myself gazing at a jagged wedge of overcast sky.

That is what I fell through, I thought. Like Alice down the rabbit hole. *Oh, my ears and whiskers, I shall be late!* Except that there was no rabbit. I wasn't following anyone. What was I doing? I was going to the edge to look over and to see — to see —

"Are you alive?" the voice asked again, and it was a voice I knew.

This time I managed to answer.

"Yes, Jeff, I am."

There was silence. Then he said incredulously, "Laurie?"

"Yes."

"Laurie? Is it really Laurie?" The hand explored the outline of my face, moving across my forehead down the ridge of my nose. It touched my lips. "I'm hallucinating, right? I knew that would happen soon. What's next, pink elephants?"

"You're not funny," I said weakly. "I fell. I went on the rocks, like you said not to, and I stepped in a crevice. We ought to be dead, oughtn't we?"

"Probably," Jeff said. "My God, Laurie, I've been so alone here. It's been so cold. Is it really you?" The question came out like a sob.

I managed to raise a hand and take hold of his.

"I can't think now," I said. "We'll talk in a little while. Okay?"

"Okay," Jeff said. "Sure, that's okay. We've got all the time in the world."

So I let my eyes fall closed, and thought about mermaids with their long wet hair streaming over their shoulders like seaweed as they glided effortlessly through the water-filled passages of their underworld home. They were just as Megan had described, and I let myself glide with them. Perhaps I slept a little. Or perhaps this time I did lose consciousness, for I was not aware of how much time was passing.

When I opened my eyes again, something had changed. My mind was focusing more sharply. I tightened my grasp on Jeff's hand, and he returned the pressure.

"Thank God," he said huskily. "I thought you might be out of it for keeps."

"No, I'm awake."

"How badly hurt are you? Can you sit up?"

"I can try."

"See if you can move closer. The ledge here is wider. There's less danger of slipping off."

The idea of falling farther was terrifying enough to have driven me to try anything. Bracing for the effort, I began to drag myself slowly into a sitting position. Immediately, I realized that the pain that had seemed to be everywhere was concentrated in my right shoulder. I paused, resting my weight for a moment on my left elbow, and then continued to pull myself erect.

I heard someone making a moaning sound, and then realized that it was coming from me.

"Is it that bad?" Jeff asked softly.

"My shoulder hurts. I can't tell more than that. What about you?"

"I think I broke a leg," Jeff said. "Yesterday it hurt like hell. I didn't think I could stand it. Now, though, it's gotten sort of numb."

"You've got to have a doctor!"

"A doctor? Laurie, come off it."

"If a broken bone isn't set, it grows back crooked."

I thought I was making such perfect sense that I could not understand the reason for his silence.

Then Jeff said quietly, "I'm not going to be walking on that leg. We're not getting out of here."

"Of course we are," I said. "We didn't fall into the middle of the earth. It can't be more than twelve feet or so to that hole up there, and we're no more than fifty yards from the back of Cliff House. When I don't come to dinner, my folks will look for me, and they'll lower ropes or something and get us out."

"Sure, they'll hunt, but what makes you think they'll find us?"

"We'll make them," I said. "We'll yell till they hear us."

"Don't you think I've tried that? Listen to my voice. There's nothing left of it. All last night I lay here yelling my head off — to you — to my dad — to God Himself, and a lot of good it did. The surf is so loud that somebody would have to be directly over us to be able to hear. As for our being near Cliff House, how does that help? You can't see the opening in the rocks from there or even from the end of the path. You have to be right on top of it. You know that. You wouldn't have fallen otherwise."

"My folks will find us," I said stubbornly. "You don't know my father."

"Maybe not, but I do know when something is impossible." He shifted his position. "Do you think you can move closer?"

"I can if you help me."

"I'm afraid I'll hurt you."

"I'll be okay. Just watch out for my right shoulder."

I leaned toward him, and he put his arm around me and began to draw me gently along the rock shelf. A shaft of pain shot through me, and I pressed my lips tightly together to keep from crying out.

Jeff must have heard my indrawn breath, because he hesitated. "You're sure you're okay?"

"I'm sure. We've almost made it."

"All right, then. Grit your teeth." He hauled me over the rest of the way, and I settled against him with a sigh of relief. The idea of sliding off into that dark hole was more horrifying than any nightmare I could imagine.

Now that I was beside him I could feel how cold he was. His body was shaking, and I could hear the chatter of his

160

teeth. I managed to turn enough so that I could get my left hand around to undo the snaps on his jacket. Then I unsnapped my own. I slipped my arms inside the opening in his parka and leaned against his chest so that the warmth of my body would be transferred to his. I could feel the thud of his heart so strong and close that it seemed to belong to both of us. The violence of his shivering frightened me, for it was beyond anything I had ever experienced. No wonder his leg was numb! His circulation must have been almost nonexistent!

"How did it happen?" I asked him. "Why were you out here?"

"You don't know?" He seemed genuinely surprised.

"Of course I don't. How could I?"

"Well, weren't you there?"

"There?" I repeated blankly. "Where? What are you talking about?"

"You were there. Out on the rocks." He paused, and then with less certainty he added, "I *think* you were there. Things are getting hazy. I remember seeing you there, because — I wouldn't have gone there otherwise, would I?"

"I understand," I said. "You saw a girl on the rocks. A girl who looked exactly like me except for her eyes."

"I didn't get close enough to see her eyes," Jeff said. "I was halfway to her when I fell. She was calling to me. I couldn't hear her voice over the sound of the waves, but I could see her lips moving, and she was waving me toward her. It was you. Or am I crazy? It had to be you, but if it was, then — then — you'd have known, and you wouldn't have fallen yourself. My mind's groggy. I can't make sense."

"It wasn't me," I said.

"There's somebody, then, who looks like you. That girl Ahearn saw on the beach. It's that person, right?"

"Her name is Lia," I told him.

"I'm awfully sleepy." He was losing his grasp on the conversation. I could feel him drifting off. "Don't let me fall."

"I won't." I was afraid for him to sleep, and afraid for him not to. His shivering had lessened, which must have meant he was warmer. "Have you slept at all?"

"I was scared to. I knew I'd roll off. Do you think if I sleep now you could hang onto me?"

"For a while," I said. "Then I'm going to wake you."

"Just for a minute," he mumbled and was asleep immediately.

He slept so hard that it was like holding a dead person, except that I could feel the slow, continuous pounding of his heart. My own mind was awake and churning, far more alert than it had been before. How could I have failed to guess that it was Lia who had arranged this? Hadn't she warned me? Hadn't she ordered me straight out, "Tell Jeff not to come here! Tell him never to come again!" I had not obeyed, so this was to be my punishment. Jeff was right; it was planned that we would die here. And no one would find us or learn what had occurred. It would be one of those unsolved mysteries — "Two Teenagers Disappear Within Twenty-four-Hour Period From Island Off Coast of New England."

Why would she do this? That was the mystery. The whole thing was so senseless. There was no reason. There was nothing for Lia to gain by taking my life, and as for

Jeff — what was he to Lia? Until this moment he had not even been aware of her existence.

An hour — or more, or less — moved by; there was no way of knowing exactly. Then, just as I was thinking I ought to try to wake him, Jeff stirred and said, "I love you." At first I thought I had not heard him right, but he continued drowsily, "I used to lie awake at night and think how it would be to hold you. So, now I know. Crazy, right?"

"No, it's not crazy," I said gently.

"It is crazy, because I thought it would be great. Instead, it's like saying good-bye."

"It's not good-bye." But I was beginning to believe that it was.

"Laurie —" He seemed to shake himself more awake. "We were riding back from school one day, and it was cold, and your hair was blowing. I had my arm up along the back of the seat. I almost put it down around you. Then I thought, no, I won't try that here. It's got to be in the dark when she won't have to look at my face."

"It wouldn't have mattered," I said. "I'm used to your face."

"Nobody gets used to that. My own mom — you know what she said? 'I can't take it,' she said. 'It makes me sick to see him like this. Can't they do something?' And the doctor said, 'Maybe. After a couple of years, maybe, something can be done. We'll see at that time. What sort of medical coverage do you carry?' So she said, 'I think he'd better live on the island.'"

"Oh, Jeff," I said. "How awful."

"She didn't put it quite like that. She said, 'I think he

should live with his dad. A teenage boy needs a man for a role model.' She never thought that before. She always said just the opposite — that my dad was a lousy example for me. What it came down to was that she couldn't stand to look at me."

"I can look at you," I said. "Your face is your face. It's part of you."

"That's what Helen said. She said, 'Tell Laurie how you feel.' And I told her, 'Helen, old buddy, you've got to be nuts. She'd freak out.' And Helen said — she said —"

He was slipping away again. A wave of panic swept over me. Somehow I knew that if he left this time it would be for good.

"Stay awake," I told him urgently. "You've got to stay awake. We're going to get out of here."

"There's no way."

"There is a way! There is!"

It happened so suddenly that I could not believe it. One moment I was with Jeff on the rock ledge, and an instant later I was floating above him. The darkness had not lessened, yet I could see everything — the boy with the scarred face — the girl with her head on his shoulder. I knew that girl was Laurie Stratton, yet she was someone completely apart from me. I was detached, clear of entrapments, moving upward. Rising like smoke, like the ocean mists, like a drop of water being drawn by the sun, I moved through the opening above me. And I was free!

Free in a world of sky! It stretched in all directions. I could rise into it, if I wished, and keep on rising. I could become part of it and expand beyond into nothing and everything. The evening air should have been cold, but I did not feel it. I could see straight through the gray clouds to the sun. Up I rose, until the clouds lay far behind me. The wind came singing, and it carried a million stories. Lia had been right, there were no words here. There did not have to be. All things were known and understood. A gull screamed somewhere miles away, and I knew. A child cried on the mainland, and I heard. I was apart from the earth, yet everything on it was mine.

There were far places waiting, strange voices calling, yet I could not resist one look at the familiar. I moved to the level of the rocks in front of Cliff House and immediately saw Neal.

He had been out riding, and his hair was ruffled by the wind so that it looked like chicken feathers. He was whistling as he wheeled his bike along the path in the direction of the shed. Halfway there he stopped, bent over, and seemed to be inspecting his front tire. Then he slowly straightened and stood without moving, leaning on the handlebars, his eyes unfocused and dreamy.

He seemed to be staring straight through me out to sea. Then, suddenly, he blinked.

"Laurie?" It was more of a question than a statement. "Laurie?"

He stood there a moment longer without moving, his face creased with puzzlement. Then, abruptly, he whirled and, letting the bike fall to the ground, began to run toward the house.

"Laurie!" another voice called. This was no question but a cry of desperation. Not one of the family, but still, a voice I knew, a voice that drew me. Who — why — ?

And then I remembered.

It was like awaking from a dream of flying.

I'm here, Jeff! I'm here! I answered silently.

I slipped downward, the rocks offering no resistance, and felt myself caught as though by some gigantic magnetic force. I could not have fought it if I had tried. With a wrenching jerk I was snapped into the body of a girl named Laurie Stratton, and *became* Laurie Stratton.

"Don't die and leave me!" Jeff whispered.

"I won't. I'm back. It's all okay." It was all I could tell him. I clung to him tightly there in the darkness until my father's head and shoulders appeared above us silhouetted against the sky.

CHAPTER 15

THEY TOOK US UP ON ROPES. IT WAS easier on Jeff than on me because he was unconscious. There was a whole rescue squad assembled, and Tommy Burbank was lowered to help us. He kept muttering, "Damn, Laurie, you've been living out here your whole life. How could you get into such a damned-fool mess?" By the time they got the harnesses down, Jeff was no longer with it, so he could be strapped in and raised without commotion. As for me, I screamed my head off.

The thing that made this so ridiculous was that I did not turn out to be all that badly injured. We were both taken to St. Joseph's, but I was released that same evening. My shoulder was bruised and swollen, but there was nothing major wrong. Jeff's left leg was broken, and he was suffering from exposure. So I went home, and Jeff didn't, and it was days before I saw him again.

In truth, it was days before I saw anything. The pain of my shoulder was out of all proportion to the seriousness of the injury, and the doctor prescribed some pills that really wiped me out. I remember little about that period, but the few memories I do have are of murmuring, "Mother?" and of her sticking another pill into my mouth.

"Sleep, honey," she kept saying, and the words became a singsong melody at the core of my consciousness — "Sleep, honey — sleep and get better."

So I slept. And when eventually I came up from the depths, it was as though I had been away on a long trip.

"Jeff?" I asked. "How's Jeff?"

"Better than he should be, considering," Dad said. "He's supposed to come home tomorrow."

"How bad is his leg?"

"That was a simple fracture, but the kid nearly froze. Do you realize he was stuck down that hole for almost twenty-four hours? Another night would have finished him. More than that, if Neal hadn't seen you fall, you could have died with him."

"Neal saw me fall?" I repeated.

"He was walking his bike up the path and saw you on the rocks. The fog was rolling in, and at first he thought it was an illusion. Then he realized it really was you, and an instant later you vanished. It scared him to death."

"So that's how you came to find us," I said.

"Neal rushed in and got me, and the two of us checked out the place where he'd seen you standing. There was that gaping hole leading down to nowhere. It was like a miracle when I heard your voice calling up to me."

"Whatever led you to go out there in the first place?" Mother asked. "You knew how dangerous it was."

"I found the books Jeff brought over the night before," I told her. "They were there at the end of the path. All I could think was that he might have gone out to the edge and slipped and fallen."

"If that had been the case, you wouldn't have found him," Dad said grimly. "He would have been long gone, washed around the point."

I shuddered. "I wasn't thinking that clearly. When I saw the books —" I paused. Where were the books? I had forgotten all about them. "They must still be out there," I said.

"Neal brought them in," Mother said. "I think they're in the living room."

She was right, they were. The cover of the red one was warped from dampness, but other than that they were both intact. I spent the next two days reading.

I started with the section Jeff had described on the phone about the experiments that had been run on a man named Ingo Swann at Stanford Research Center. Aside from his performances in the laboratory identifying objects on a raised platform, Swann was said to have demonstrated his ability to project himself to distant locations simply by being given their longitudes and latitudes. Upon his return he would prove he had been there by sketching the terrain. On one occasion he had returned from an astral trip to a supposedly uninhabited island in the southern part of the Indian Ocean to report that there had been people there speaking French. Investigation later revealed that the French government had built a meteorological station on that island.

Swann's case history was followed by others, equally amazing. A tremendous number of people had testified over the years to having had out-of-body experiences. "In many cases," the book reported, "these subjects started having such experiences in childhood and grew up assuming that everyone else did also. When they mentioned their astral trips to family and friends it was done so casually that listeners thought that they were describing dreams."

One chapter in the red book was devoted to ancient history. There were photographs of paintings that had been found in Egyptian tombs that showed a second body hovering over the first one. Ancient Chinese and Indian manuscripts were cited, describing men who routinely sent their spiritual bodies on "heavenly flights," and there was one section that elaborated on the Eastern religions in which lamas and monks were required to leave their bodies as part of their religious training.

But the thing that caught and held me was one short paragraph that referred to "the Indians of North America, the Algonquin, Shoshone, and Navajo in particular, who seem to have an innate understanding of how to use their astral powers." I read that sentence several times. I remembered Helen's casual comment that "the medicine men could do it whenever they wanted, and some of the others too."

And now I was among that number.

The day I finished the second book I phoned Jeff. Mr. Rankin said that he could not come to the phone but that he would call me back. The call never came.

The following morning I struggled into my parka, tucked the two books under my arm, and walked the two miles to the Rankin cottage. I rang the bell, and Jeff's voice called out something which I took to be "Come in." Whether it was or not, I shoved open the door and stepped into a room that was about as void of personality as any I had ever entered. There were chairs and a couch covered in some sort of drab brown material, and the curtains at the windows were a lighter shade of brown with a checkerboard design running through them. There was nothing on the walls, not a picture or even a calendar, and there were no plants or cushions or magazines or anything else to show that two people made their home there.

If this was a "bachelor pad," I thought, glancing about me, I hoped Neal would marry directly out of high school.

Jeff was seated in an armchair with his leg in a cast propped up on a coffee table. A television set stood against the wall directly across from him blaring out the sound track from an old movie in which masked bandits were shooting each other off rooftops.

I started to say, "Hi," and then realized that I wouldn't be able to hear my own voice.

Jeff glanced up at me with an expression that made me wonder if he was going to sit there and let the thing keep running. Then, with apparent reluctance, he pushed one of the buttons on the remote control panel in his lap, and the set sputtered into silence.

"Hello," I said. "How's the leg?"

"Broken," Jeff said shortly. "How's the shoulder?" His eyes were cool and uncommunicative with that distant, closed-in look that they held so often.

"It's better," I said. "I got off easier than you did."

He didn't invite me to sit down, but I did so anyway. The sofa was just as uncomfortable as I had thought it would be.

"You don't act like you're very happy to see me," I said.

"So what are you here for anyway? I'd have thought you'd have had enough of my company to last a lifetime."

"You didn't return my phone call," I said accusingly.

"I didn't have anything to say."

"Maybe I *did* have something to say. Did that occur to you?"

"Not really," Jeff said. "I figured you were doing the duty thing."

"Well, I wasn't. I needed to talk to you, but there's no sense even trying if you're going to be like this. What are you mad about?"

"I'm not mad," he said. "It's just —" His eyes shifted away from mine, and he drew a deep breath. "Look, no guy likes to know some girl saw him make a fool of himself."

"You didn't do that."

"Don't give me that. I was *there,* remember?" His voice was brusque and embarrassed. "So, what was it you wanted to talk about?"

I don't know what he expected, but I'm sure it was not what he got.

"Astral projection," I told him.

"I don't know anything about that. Only what I read in those books Helen bought." He paused, frowned. "Are those the books you've got there? Where did you find them?"

"Out by the path where you left them," I said. "Neal brought them in, and I've been reading them."

"Weird, right?"

"Yes, sure, but — Jeff, do you believe in it?"

"I don't know," he said carefully. "A week ago I'd have said 'crazy.' But after reading those case studies — well, there's got to be something. I mean, they were documented and everything. What do you think?"

"It's real," I said. "I know, because I've done it."

Jeff was silent a moment. Then he surprised me by nodding.

"So that's what happened," he said.

"Yes, that's what happened. Neal saw me in some sort of form out over the rocks. He got Dad, and the two of them came out and found us."

"I thought you'd died," Jeff said. "That's when I started freaking out. You seemed to stop breathing, and I couldn't find a heartbeat. One minute it was you, and the next it was like I was hanging onto an empty shell. How did you do it?"

"I don't know," I told him.

"You've *got* to know! The people in those books knew!"

"They didn't all know the first time it happened," I said. "In a lot of the cases people projected at a time of shock, like during an accident. They didn't even know what was happening until it was over and they were back again."

"Yeah, you're right, I guess." He was regarding me with a combination of awe and amazement. "What did it feel like?"

"I don't know how to describe it exactly. Like — being free. Like not being tied to anything or anyone, just able to go. The thing is, I didn't know where to go or how to get there. I wasn't in control of it the way Lia is."

"Lia? That girl who looks like you? She can do this too?"

"That girl's my sister," I said. "I want to tell you about her."

The strange thing was that he didn't disbelieve me. He sat through the story in silence, and when I was finished he had only one question.

"Why?"

"Why, what?"

"Why does she hate you like that? It's not like you'd done anything. It's she who came to find you, not the other way around. The way you tell it, she's been slowly moving in on you. It was first little things, like appearing on the beach where Ahearn could see her, and then in your dreams, and then when you were awake, until now it's like she's trying to get you separated from everybody who's important to you."

"It's true," I agreed. "I don't have friends anymore. I don't quite know how that happened. It was my own doing, wasn't it? I mean, I let them all go."

"Because she was absorbing you?"

"I don't know," I said, confused. "Lia didn't actually do anything."

"Except to me," Jeff said. "She tried to kill me, remember? And what about Helen?"

"You think Lia caused Helen's accident?" The moment I voiced the question, I knew the answer. The surprising thing was that I had not realized it much sooner. "Of course, she caused it. She lured Helen into the park that night. She got her there the same way she got you out onto those rocks."

"By being you," Jeff said.

"Yes, by being me." Suddenly I was shaking. I was colder than I had been in the underground cavern. The full horror of the situation swept upon me, accentuated by my own utter helplessness.

"What is she going to do next?" I asked. "How can I predict or prevent it? I don't know where she comes from. There's no way to find her. I don't know what she's after or what her plans are. She comes and goes when she chooses, and I don't even get to see her unless she wants me to."

"After this long a time, you've got to have found out something," Jeff said. "Is there any pattern? When does she visit you?"

"Whenever she wants to. In the afternoons or in the evenings. When I'm in bed at night."

"What about mornings?"

Had she come in the mornings? I tried to remember. She had never been there in my bedroom when I awakened. Nor had there been instances at school when someone accused me of having been somewhere that I wasn't. The people who had reported such instances — Gordon, Natalie, Mary Beth, my brother and sister — had all of them seen the person they thought was Laurie Stratton during the later hours of the day.

"Jeff, I've thought of something," I said slowly. "I don't know if this means anything, but Lia didn't know about Mrs. DeWitt."

"You mean Edna DeWitt from the village?"

"She cleans for us Thursdays. Once I mentioned her name to Lia, and she didn't seem to know a thing about her."

"Mrs. DeWitt works mornings?"

"Half-days. She leaves by two. She likes to be home when her children get out of school. A couple of times she's come on other days also, like when it was time to do a big project like wash the windows, but those were mornings too."

"So we do know something," Jeff said with satisfaction. "We know that whatever Lia's physical life may consist of, there's something in it that keeps her occupied in the mornings."

"Perhaps she goes to school," I suggested.

"That's sure possible. She's exactly your age, so she ought to be a senior. What else can you come up with? Did she talk a lot about one specific area of the country?"

"Our mother moved to Gallup, New Mexico, when she left the reservation," I said. "That's where the agency was that I was adopted from. Lia never indicated that they moved again, so when our mother died and Lia was placed in a foster home, we can probably assume it was in that general area."

"So you've got a place to aim for." Jeff was beginning to sound excited.

"To aim for? What do you mean?"

"If Lia could find you here on Brighton Island, what's to keep you from finding her out in New Mexico? You're one up on her. At least you've got a pretty good idea of what part of the country she's in. When she went searching for you she was coming out of nowhere. When your folks adopted you, they were living in New York City."

"I can't do it," I said.

"Why not? You did it once, didn't you? Now you've had the experience, a second time ought to be easy!"

"If I did manage to leave my body, I wouldn't know how to direct myself."

"You could learn, couldn't you? Lia did."

"What if she doesn't let me?"

"How can she stop you?"

"I don't know," I said. "That's the thing — I don't know anything. Helen didn't want me to try it. The whole idea scared her. She seemed to think that my doing it would be dangerous."

"But you *have* done it," Jeff said. "And nothing awful happened. In fact, neither of us would be alive now if you hadn't gotten help. The way it looks to me, Laurie, is that the dangerous thing would be for you not to try to get control of this — this — gift, or whatever you want to call it. If you don't, you're at Lia's mercy, and if what she pulled last week is an indication, there's not going to be much mercy to spare."

"I don't understand why she hates me," I told him helplessly. " 'We are the two sides of a coin —' "

"The dark and the light side."

"Coins aren't made that way," I said.

"But people are."

We sat quiet, both contemplating the statement.

Then Jeff gave a short, wry laugh. "Yeah, I know what you're thinking. I got them both, right? A face split down the center. Which side is your Lia after, the good or the bad one?"

"I hate it when you talk like that," I said. "I hate it when you *think* like that. It doesn't matter. I told you that before. It doesn't matter, Jeff."

"You said that because you thought we were dying."

"And you said you loved me because you thought we were dying?" I threw the challenge back at him.

"Yeah, I guess I did. *If* I said it. I don't remember it."

"You said it."

"I was in shock, right? I was delirious. I might have said all kinds of crazy stuff, but it didn't mean anything."

"You said you loved me," I said.

"You didn't hear me right. A guy with a face like mine doesn't go around saying that. What kind of girl would want to hear it? She'd have to be an idiot."

"There are a few idiots floating around."

"Like who, for instance?"

"Oh, stop the game-playing, Jeff Rankin." Suddenly I was so angry and frustrated I wanted to hit him. "What you said, you said. What you meant, you meant. Do whatever you want to about it. I wish I'd never come over here."

I was halfway to the door, when he called out, "Laurie?"

"What?" I said without turning.

"Come back a minute."

I had stopped in midflight, and now I turned slowly to face him. I stared at that face, that comic-book face, that was just as he had described it. It was something out of Dick Tracy. It was sad, and it was awful, and it was brave, and it was beautiful, and I loved it.

"What is it?" I asked.

"I was lying," Jeff said. "I do remember. I remember everything."

"And?"

He grimaced. "Don't make it tough on me, Laurie. Okay?"

"Okay," I said. It was that simple.

I went over to him and put my arms around him, and he pulled me down onto his lap on top of that wretched cast, and it was like sitting on a stovepipe. And we both started laughing. And he kissed me.

It was the end of one chapter of our relationship and the beginning of another.

CHAPTER 16

On New Year's Eve, Darlene Briggs gave a party. To my surprise, I found myself invited. It seemed that Tommy had bragged enough about his involvement in the rescue mission so that everybody on Brighton Island was dying to pump for details.

"Can I bring a date?" I asked when Darlene phoned me with her invitation.

"I don't think you'll need to, Laurie," she said. "You may not have heard, but Gordon and Joyce broke up over Christmas. He's going to be coming stag, and he made a big point of asking me if you were invited."

"And Joyce?" I couldn't help asking.

"She's not on the guest list. It's just too awkward. She's never really been one of the crowd, you know. She got included in things because she was dating Gordon."

"I understand," I said. I did understand, all too well. "I don't think I can make it. I have a date already. But thank you for inviting me."

Jeff and I saw the New Year in at Cliff House playing

Monopoly with my parents and the children. It was one of the nicest New Year's Eves I can remember.

New Year's Day was quiet and pleasant without much happening. Family life went on as usual, with Dad at the typewriter and Mother up in her studio preparing a canvas for her next painting. Mrs. Coleson had been so delighted with her Christmas present that she wanted a second oil framed identically so they could balance each other on either side of the fireplace. Meg went off to play at a friend's house, and Neal and I dismantled the Christmas tree and packed away the ornaments. This was a chore I usually found depressing, but this year it was almost a relief to officially place Christmas behind us and close the book upon a season that had been more traumatic than joyful.

I can't pinpoint the time it happened, but somewhere along about the middle of the afternoon I began to have the sensation that someone was watching. The feeling was not unfamiliar, but I had been without it for a week and had begun to dare to hope it was gone forever. There had been no sign of Lia since the day before Christmas. Things had changed since then. I was no longer trusting and no longer isolated. Jeff and I were a team. There were two of us, united. That knowledge should have been enough to cause Lia to draw back and reconsider the wisdom of continuing her invasion.

While Neal was carting the boxes of ornaments down to the storage shed, I phoned Jeff.

"She's here," I said without elaboration.

"Have you seen her?" he asked.

"No, but I sense her. It's like an aura." I struggled to find the words to explain it. "The first day she came, back in September, I felt her presence, but I didn't know what I was feeling. I told Mother, 'Someone's been in my room,' even though nothing had been disturbed. It's the same thing now, this feeling. It's like a soft, continued sound your ear doesn't register. It fills your head, but you can't hear any noise."

"If it wasn't for this cast, I'd come over," Jeff said. "There's no way I can walk that far on crutches. Dad's not here, and I can't keep asking your dad to keep chauffeuring me."

"He couldn't anyway," I said. "He's writing. And it's not like you could do anything."

"You know she's there. That's the best defense you've got," Jeff said reassuringly. "You have a handle on things. You know now that Lia's an enemy. She can't lure you or trick you, because you're onto her. And there's nothing she can do physically. She's not *there* physically."

"She's somewhere physically," I said. "That's the part that scares me. She could be thousands of miles from here or right around the corner. What if she is close by? What if one day she appears to me, and I think it's just her shadow self, and she's *real?*"

"That would be bad news," Jeff agreed. "And that's why you've got to find her."

"Helen told me —"

"You can't hide behind Helen, Laurie. Things were different then. Helen gave you the best advice she could, but there wasn't any way for her to know things would go this far."

"I can't try while she's here," I said desperately.

"No, of course you can't. But in the morning — you're safe in the mornings."

"How do we *know* that?"

"We can't know anything for sure," Jeff said. "We can just do our best with what we have to go on. In the morning, Laurie. Promise?"

"All right, I promise."

Was it my imagination, or was the room filled suddenly with silent laughter?

Somehow, I got through the remainder of the afternoon and the evening that followed. We ate an early supper, and the kids fell into bed soon afterward, exhausted from having stayed up the night before to see the New Year in, and groaning with thoughts of school the following day. Mother went to bed with a book, and Dad went back to his typewriter. Quiet settled over Cliff House, and with that quiet the nightmare feeling that soon it would be broken by something I did not want to hear.

But this did not happen. Lia did not appear to me that night. I lay awake for hours, rereading the books that Helen had bought for me, trying to absorb as much information as possible. Both books referred to something they called the "astral cord" which serves as a connection between the free-floating astral self and the body. This cord, as they described it, works like a magnet, losing strength as the astral self pulls farther and farther away and regaining it when the soul-self moves closer. "In the immediate proximity of the body," one book said, "the tug of the cord becomes so intense that the two selves are rejoined with what one subject described as 'a sharp click' and another as 'a jolt.' The astral cord remains intact no matter how far it is stretched and can be severed only by death."

All this made good sense to me when I reviewed my own experience. It had been when I had returned to the cavern to look in upon Jeff that I had been jerked forcibly back into my body. On recalling the situation, I doubted that I would have been able to resist if I had wanted to.

So, at least I know that I can never be lost, I thought. No matter how far I go, I will be able to follow the cord back. It was a comforting realization. The worst of my fantasies had been getting so far from Cliff House that I would not know how to return.

I read on and on until the words on the page began to become blurred and meaningless, and then, half fearfully, half defiantly, I reached over and snapped off the bedside light.

The room remained still and empty. The darkness was gentle.

I closed my eyes and, with a sigh of relief, slid into sleep.

I awoke very early. The light of the sun was barely starting to filter up from the under side of the earth and send streaks into the sky to reflect in the water. I lay in bed, gazing out through the glass doors and watching the clouds turn from gray to lavender to pink to rose in readiness for an explosion into morning.

It's time, I thought. I gave Jeff my promise.

I had promised I would try. I had not promised results. I had tried so often before and gotten nowhere that I had little confidence that this attempt would be different. Still, I did know now what it was I was striving for. I knew how it felt to release my hold on the earth. I did not have to imagine, I could *remember,* and when I closed my eyes in concentration I was returning to a realm in which I had already been.

I was there on the bed; then, I was over it. The thing happened so quickly it was like flinging myself off the end of a diving board. I took one great leap, and was free.

Beneath me lay the motionless figure of a dark-haired girl

who seemed to be sleeping. I gazed down at her with little interest. That is my body, I told myself, but it could have been anyone for all the emotion it aroused. Then I was higher, over Cliff House, looking down on the rooftop, and higher still so that the whole of Brighton Island lay spread below me. I was over water, and then over clouds, I saw the edge of the sun curve over the eastern horizon, and I was traveling faster than it was. If I kept rising, I would be above the sun and beyond it, moving faster and farther until I became a part of the great, incredible forever that lay past everything.

But that was not my destination.

I was going to Helen.

I had wondered how I would find her. I need not have worried. It simply — happened. As the flight from my body had happened. I was drawn instinctively to where I wanted to be.

I was in a hospital corridor. Not too quiet a corridor. One set of nurses was moving in, and another set leaving. People were checking charts and hunting up raincoats.

"Horrid weather out," one incoming woman commented in a soft, slow drawl, and another, preparing to leave, said, "What can we expect in January?"

I was among them, but no one could see me. My father had told me once about a comic strip, popular when he was a boy, that had been one of the springboards that had led him into fantasy and science fiction.

"It was called 'Invisible Scarlet O'Neal,' " he said. "There was this girl named Scarlet who could press a nerve in her wrist and make herself invisible. Then she'd go running around, eavesdropping and playing practical jokes and catching criminals. I was fascinated. My own wrist was one huge bruise from all the digging around I did trying to locate that nerve."

Now, it was I who was "Invisible Scarlet." How incredible that these people did not see me when I was so definitely there!

I moved down the corridor, glancing through open doors into the rooms of strangers. Most were sleeping, but there were some who were awake. One man was smoking a cigarette, and an elderly woman had her TV set on. So occupied was I with looking for a splash of carrot-colored hair against a pillow, that I did not see the two orderlies until they were on top of me. I jumped aside, but not quickly enough to avoid the bed they were wheeling. The edge of it swung into my hip and passed through it. I felt nothing, and the men continued to walk at their same rate of speed, taking the bed on down the length of the hall and through swinging doors at its end.

A moment later a nurse came hurrying toward me. This time I made no attempt to move out of her path, and we passed through each other as though one of us were made of air.

A door to my left beckoned. I could not have said why, but I knew without a doubt that the room beyond was Helen's.

So, I've found you at last! I moved through the doorway to stand beside her bed.

Helen was lying on her back with her arms at her sides. Her eyes were closed, and she was thinner than I remembered. Her breathing was slow and steady, and her face was pale beneath its freckles. I don't know what it was I had expected — bandages — a respirator — but I was surprised by the normalcy of her appearance. She might have been sleeping, instead of in a coma that had lasted for weeks.

I'm sorry, I thought. Helen, I am so sorry! I'm the one who brought Lia into your life. You tried to warn me. It isn't fair that you should be the one to suffer.

"Helen, you have a visitor!"

The voice, coming so unexpectedly from behind me, startled me so that I jumped with the instinctive guilt that I would have felt as a physical intruder.

A plump, round-faced nurse came bustling into the room. Behind her was Mr. Tuttle.

"Wake up, Helen," the woman said. "Your daddy's here."

Wake up! I thought. How can she demand such a thing!

To my astonishment, Helen's eyelids quivered. Her head moved on the pillow, and her mouth opened in a yawn.

"Hello, baby," said Mr. Tuttle. "I hate to wake you, but I'm on the way to the airport. I didn't want to leave without saying good-bye."

"'Morning, Dad," Helen said drowsily. "Where is it you're going?"

"Shiprock, New Mexico," her father said. "Remember, I told you they had a sudden opening for a teacher who speaks Navajo?"

"That's right. You did tell me," Helen said. "It's funny. I had this thing in my mind that we were going to New England. Didn't you say once that you wanted me to have my senior year in an eastern school?"

"Your mother and I changed our minds," Mr. Tuttle told her. "We decided that wouldn't be our sort of place."

"We were going to see snow. We talked about that. I've never seen snow, and you said —" She paused, as though struggling to get the thought clear in her mind. "You said, 'Everybody should have a chance to experience a real winter once.'"

"I know, baby, and we will," her father said. "There's snow in the mountains of New Mexico. They even have skiing. You'd like to learn to ski, wouldn't you?"

"Sure, I guess." She smiled at him. It was a weak smile, but it brought with it a flash of the Helen I knew. "When do Mom and I get to come?"

"It'll be a while yet. The doctors have to give us the go-ahead."

"Was I hurt badly?" Helen asked the question with more interest than concern.

"Badly enough to scare us. We want you completely well before we go taking you off someplace. You keep getting better the way you've been doing, and we'll be together in no time. Meanwhile, I'll find us a house and get our stuff shipped out."

"Will Mom be in later today?"

"She'll be here for visiting hours, like she always is. They let me in out of hours just to say good-bye." He bent and kissed her lightly on the forehead. "You get well fast, all right? I'm going to be lonesome out there without my womenfolk."

"I will, Dad. I promise. As fast as I can."

She smiled at him again, and the expression held until he was gone from the room. Then the smile disappeared, and her brows drew together in a puzzled frown.

"Mrs. Jensen," she said slowly, "how long have I been here at Duke?"

"A couple of weeks, dear," the nurse responded pleasantly. She had left the room briefly during Mr. Tuttle's visit and was back now, refilling the water pitcher on the table by the bed.

"And before that, was I in another hospital?"

"Yes, they transferred you here from someplace. I don't know where. I wasn't working on this ward when you arrived."

"Was it a hospital in Arizona?"

"I told you, dear, I don't know. Dr. Cohn will be making his rounds in a little bit, and you can ask him. Or your mother will be here for visiting hours."

"It doesn't matter, I guess. It's just that it's a weird feeling not being able to remember." She sighed and let her eyes fall closed.

"Now don't you go dozing off, Miss Sleepyhead," the nurse said playfully. "Breakfast will be along any minute now, and you'll just have to wake right up again."

Breakfast. It would be breakfast time at Cliff House also.

The children would be up and dressed by now, and *I —*

I need to get back! And even as I thought it, I was there. The return was so fast that I was not aware of what was happening. There was an instant of speed and light, the sensation of being yanked through space by some tremendous force, as though I were attached to the end of a gigantic rubber band that had been stretched almost to its snapping point and was then released. The world shot by beneath me in a crazy blur of land and water half concealed by clouds, and my soul-self met my body with such an impact that I gasped aloud.

I was lying on my bed, and someone was shaking me so hard my teeth were rattling.

"Laurie," Neal was pleading frantically, "please, wake up!"

"Don't!" I mumbled. "Take it easy, Neal! You're hurting me."

"I've never seen anybody sleep like that." There was relief in his voice as he released his grip on my shoulders. "It was like you weren't even breathing. You scared me."

"Don't worry," I said. "I'm here. I'm back again."

"Back again?" Neal repeated in bewilderment.

"I mean, I'm awake. I'm back in the waking world." I sat up in bed, thrust back the covers, and slid my feet over the side. "Run along and let me get dressed, okay? I'll be down to breakfast in a minute."

"You better hurry or you won't make the ferry," Neal said. "Is Jeff going to school today?"

"I think so. His father's going to drive him down to the landing, and I can carry his books to classes for him."

He'd better come, I thought, because I have a lot to tell him! And I don't want to have to wait until after school to do it.

CHAPTER 17

JEFF WAS AT THE LANDING WHEN THE KIDS and I arrived, but there was no opportunity to talk in private. There was time only for us to board and find ourselves seats inside. The weather was so grim that no one wanted to ride in the open air, and with the shape he was in, Jeff could not have made it to the top deck anyway.

The crowd in the cabin welcomed us with unaccustomed enthusiasm. The fact that we were survivors of a dangerous adventure seemed to have turned us into overnight celebrities. Everybody had questions. How had the accident occurred? How far had we fallen? What had it been like to be trapped in such a situation? How had we been rescued?

"It was hairy," Tommy Burbank kept saying over and over, resentful that his part in the drama was not getting full recognition. "I was the one they lowered in. It was black as pitch down there. Rankin was out cold, and Laurie was hysterical."

"My shoulder was injured," I said. "I thought the harness was going to wrench it out of the socket. Jeff was unconscious by then. He'd been there a lot longer than I and was nearly frozen."

"So, what was he doing there anyway?" Gordon had managed somehow to claim the seat on my right, and the old note of possessiveness was in his voice. "Are you in the habit of hanging around Cliff House at night, Rankin?"

"I was out there picking flowers for May baskets," Jeff said coolly.

"Cut the smart stuff. I asked you a simple question."

"And I gave you a simple answer."

"By 'simple' I didn't mean 'stupid,'" Gordon said. "Christmas Eve isn't exactly the time most people decide to go hiking on the rocks."

"I invited him, Gordon," I said. "He was coming over for dinner."

"To your place?" Gordon sounded incredulous.

"To my girlfriend's place. Got any objections?" Jeff grinned. It was the old, cocky grin of three years before, except that now it affected only the good half of his face.

Gordon's mouth opened and closed again without a sound coming out of it.

Then, Darlene, who was seated too far away to have heard what was being said, leaned over to ask, "Does anybody have 'A' lunch this semester?" and Rennie said, "I do," and everyone began trading class schedules. With the change in topic, the conversation took off in other directions. Gordon didn't speak again for the rest of the ride.

When the ferry reached the mainland, Jeff and I held back long enough to let the others disembark ahead of us. Then he hauled himself to his feet, and I gathered up his books and my own.

"Did you see the expression on Ahearn's face?" Jeff asked.

"Yes, and I saw the look on yours, like the cat who swallowed the canary."

"Well, yeah. Probably." His eyes were twinkling. Then, abruptly, he sobered. "So what happened this morning? Did you try the projection?"

"Yes, I tried it."

"No luck, huh?"

"Luck or talent," I said. "Whichever it was, I did see Helen."

"You're kidding!" He stopped in the cabin doorway and turned to stare at me. "You were able to do it? It really worked?"

"Didn't you expect it to?" I asked. "You're the one who kept pushing me to try."

"Yeah, sure, but I thought it would take a while. The way you talked you were pretty uncertain about it."

"I shouldn't have been," I said. "I did it on the first try. It was like — like —" I wanted to put the sensation into words, but it was impossible. "It was like dreaming," I said inadequately, "except that it was real."

"Are you sure of that? If you were dreaming —"

"I wasn't. I was really there at Duke Hospital. I saw Helen. I even saw her father."

As we made our way along the sidewalk to the school, I described the visit, trying to recall every detail so that Jeff could share the experience.

"That's great news," he said when I was finished. "Is there a phone in her room?"

"A phone?" I tried to remember. "Yes, I think so. It was on the bedside table."

"Then let's call her."

"You mean, right now?" I asked. "From school? We can't make a long-distance call from the office."

"We can from the Standard station on the corner. There's a public pay phone there."

"I think it wouldn't be such a good thing," I said.

"What do you mean? You said she's okay now."

"She's conscious," I said. "But there's something I didn't tell you. She doesn't remember it, Jeff, not any of it. Not anything about New England and the time she spent here and the people she knew. I heard her talking to her father. All she can recall is that they discussed coming here. She thinks that her parents changed their minds."

"Oh, come off it!" Jeff exclaimed. "She lived here almost four months. That couldn't have been wiped away like it never happened. I'll bet all she needs is the sound of our voices to bring everything back."

"That may be so," I conceded. "Still, I don't think we should try it."

"Why not? We're her closest friends."

"But we're not doctors. We can't know for sure what the best thing for Helen is. Mr. Tuttle has my phone number. I asked him to call as soon as there was any change. The fact that he hasn't must mean that the doctors have advised against it."

"You think we should leave things as they are?" Jeff asked incredulously. "With her not remembering? That means we'll lose her forever!"

"Not necessarily," I said, trying to sound hopeful. "She may find her own way back to us. And if she doesn't, *we'll* still remember. Every time I wear the necklace she gave me, I'll think about the time —"

I broke off in mid-sentence, my hand flying instinctively to my throat. The necklace! So much had happened since Christmas morning that I had forgotten all about it. Mother had been in the process of helping me put it on when the call had come from Jeff's father.

"It's gone!" I gasped. "Helen's gift to me!"

"Relax," Jeff said. "It's not lost. I've got it at home."

"You have it? But, how —"

"The Emergency Room doctor found it caught in the zipper of my parka. I meant to tell you, but I've kept forgetting. The clasp's broken. I was going to fix it before I gave it back to you." He paused. "It's a pretty thing. Helen used to wear one like it, didn't she?"

"This is the same necklace," I said. "Her friend Luis gave it to her because she was going to take her first plane flight. Turquoise is the Navajo good-luck stone. The eagle fetish is supposed to protect the wearer against evil spirits from the skies."

"It's too bad she gave it away when she did," Jeff said wryly. "She could have used that protection."

"It's just a superstition."

"Helen believed it," Jeff said. "That must be why she gave it to you."

By now we had reached the entrance to the high school. I had to struggle to haul the heavy door open against the pressure of the mounting wind. We were enough behind the others so that the sound of the tardy bell reverberating through the empty hall came as no surprise to either of us.

I held the door for Jeff to manipulate through with his crutches. Then I released it, and the wind sent it closed with a bang.

"Evil spirits from the skies." Jeff repeated the words.

"That's what she is, Laurie. Lia's an evil spirit. You've got no choice. You have to find her, especially now that you know that it's possible."

"It's not as easy as going to Helen," I said. "I knew where Helen was."

"In the morning, you'll try?"

"Yes, I'll try," I told him. "I can't promise anything except that I'll try."

The day was hectic, as first days after vacation generally are. The confusion was accentuated by the fact that it was the start of the second semester. There were new classrooms to locate and new teachers to adjust to and a line at the book room that extended halfway down the hall.

When lunchtime came, I discovered that the story of Jeff's and my adventure had spread during the morning, and the kids from the mainland were ready to mob us for details. Even the teachers had heard about it. Mrs. Crawfield, my algebra teacher, who had been so unsympathetic about my sliding grades, detained me after class to ask if I needed extra time to complete the next assignment because "such a traumatic event can have a detrimental effect upon your ability to concentrate," and Miss Hyman, the journalism instructor, stopped me in the hall to ask if Jeff and I would collaborate on a first-person feature story for the school paper.

What with one thing and another, I was too occupied to notice what was happening beyond the classroom windows, and it was a surprise that afternoon to leave the building and find that it had begun to snow. It wasn't a light, fluffy snowfall either. The flakes were solid and sodden, plunking to earth and remaining there as a foundation for those that fell on top of them.

"Here's Helen's picture-book winter," Jeff commented with a touch of bitterness. "It's ironic that she doesn't get to see it."

The ferry ride back to the island was not a smooth one. The wind from the morning had increased in strength, and the water was choppy and speckled with whitecaps. Jeff's father was at the landing to pick him up, and I walked the distance to Cliff House, leaning into the wind, with my hands crammed into my jacket pockets.

Lia did not walk beside me this day, nor was she on the rocks or the dunes. I had not seen her for nine days, yet the closer I drew to Cliff House, the more strongly I felt her presence. As I opened the front door, the aura grew so intense that I almost expected to find her waiting for me at the top of the stairway.

But that did not occur. If she was there — and I believe she was — she did not display herself.

The remainder of the day is hazy in my memory. I did my homework. I ate dinner with the family. I can't recall what it was we talked about. I think we spent the evening playing some sort of table game, but I cannot say what it was or which of us won. I went to bed. The waves were pounding hard against the rocks. I do remember that. When I turned off the light, their thunder was magnified by the darkness, and the wind was whining around the corners of the house with a sound like a human voice begging me to open the balcony doors and let her in.

But it was not Lia who called to me, it was only the wind; and that did not frighten me. I closed my eyes and slept.

I awakened just before dawn as though I had been programmed to do so. The sky was still dark, but there was a line of pearl gray extending along the eastern horizon. I knew instinctively that Lia was no longer at Cliff House. At some point during the night she had slipped away to return to her physical self at whatever place in the world that self might be.

This time I did not pause to look behind me at the sleeping body of Laurie Stratton. I simply rose and went. It was so easy now that I wondered how I had ever found it difficult. My doubts about my ability to determine direction were immediately put to rest. My destination seemed preset. In a flash I was moving with such speed that I had no sense of distance. Somewhere ahead of me was Lia, an earthbound Lia, in solid form, and I was going to be with her.

"I'm scared for you, Laurie! It's dangerous!"

Helen's voice rang suddenly in my ears, raised in a shriek of near panic.

The memory pierced me, and I hesitated. It was for one instant only that I experienced the sensation of holding back. For one lone instant, but that was enough to divert me.

The place I reached was dark and quiet, and Lia was not there.

It was night. The sky above me was wide and clear and studded with stars. I sensed in the distance a range of mountains curving protectively around me on all sides like the rim of a bowl. I was in the valley at the bowl's center. Directly before me lay a house, low and flat-roofed, and beyond that, a garden. There was a camper in the driveway, and off to the right there was a stable that until recently had housed two horses.

How did I know this? I cannot say. I simply knew, just as I knew that Lia had once been a part of this place and of the lives of the people who lived here. She had spent nights in that camper during summer vacation trips. She had ridden one of the horses.

She had lived in this house as though it were her own.

The walls offered no resistance as I entered. I passed through them as easily as though they had been formed of air and found myself in a spacious living room. It was a lovely room, at once both comfortable and elegant. The heavy, handcarved furniture was of dark, rich wood and upholstered in rusts and golds. There was a large, circular coffee table, a color television set, and an antique upright piano. Beyond those, an Indian rug served as a wall-hanging over a long bookcase. The windowed wall facing the garden had textured draperies drawn across it to keep out the chill of the night air.

The room was not lighted, but I could see as clearly as I might have in the daytime. I could read the titles of the books on the shelves and observe the minute detail in the intricately woven pattern in the rug. On the TV set there lay some letters, evidently awaiting mailing. I could read the addresses on the envelopes. On the piano there stood a framed photograph of a smiling blonde girl with braces on her teeth. She was dressed in a riding habit, and her hair was pulled back in a high, tight ponytail.

I moved farther into the house. There were three bedrooms. In the largest of these a man and woman were sleeping. They lay close together in a queen-size bed, the woman with her cheek against the man's shoulder. The dial of the clock radio on the bedside table read five-seven. It had been later than that when I had awakened at Cliff House. In the winter the sun did not rise until nearly seven. I was momentarily bewildered by the discrepancy and then realized that I must have traveled far enough west to have passed through two time zones.

The woman made a little moaning sound. Then, suddenly, startlingly, she called out, "Kathy!"

Her body jerked convulsively, and the man came awake, rolling over to throw his arm across her.

"Kathy!" the woman cried again. "Watch out!"

"Hush, hush," the man said soothingly. "Darling, you're dreaming."

"Kathy!"

"It's a dream, just a dream." He cradled her against him and began to rock her back and forth as though she were a small child. "Hush, now. Go back to sleep."

"A dream?" the woman murmured uncertainly. "Oh, Art, it was so real!"

"I know. It always is. But it was only a dream, dear."

He continued to rock her, making the bed sway back and forth with the rhythmic motion of their bodies. She turned her face against his chest and began to cry.

I moved beyond them to the second bedroom. It was clearly uninhabited. The bed had been stripped of sheets and was covered with only a white tailored spread. The closet was so empty that there was not a thread or a shred of lint to testify to the fact that clothing had hung there.

A guest room? Perhaps. Yet, there was something about it —

I did not like that room. I moved past it to the next one. This was also empty, but it had the look of having recently been occupied by someone who was expecting to return. Cosmetics were scattered carelessly across the dressing table, and the desk was cluttered with books and papers that seemed to be connected with a homework assignment.

Several silver trophies stood on the bureau top, and over them hung a bulletin board adorned with first- and second-place ribbons from an assortment of horse shows. The skirts and dresses in the closet were outnumbered by plaid shirts and jeans. On the rumpled bed a high school yearbook lay open as though the reader had been leafing through it when she was called away to some more interesting activity.

I drew close to the bed and looked down at the row on row of pictures that constituted the "Junior Class of Sandia High." Smiling up at me from the topmost row was the girl from the gold-framed photograph in the living room. Beneath her picture a name was printed — "Katherine Abbott."

The next photo in the line might have been my own. Beneath this one the lettering read — "Lia Abbott."

CHAPTER 18

WHEN I RETURNED TO CLIFF HOUSE, I found myself confronted with a day that had not wakened. Dawn had come and gone, but the sun did not appear to have climbed into the sky. The clouds were bunched so thick and low that they completely concealed it from view. What light there was seeped through the heavy layers and emerged diluted into dishwater gray. From my bed I could see that the balcony beyond the glass doors was frosted with snow.

For a while I simply lay there, trying to get my thoughts into some kind of order. Where was it that I had been? It had been a far place, two time zones away, where winter was strange and still. The cold there had been a dry cold with a crisp, foreign feel to it, and the sky had arched above me in a canopy of stars.

I reached back with my mind, attempting to sort out the images and sensations. The house that I had visited had once been Lia's. I was as certain of that as I was of the fact that she no longer lived there. The aura of her presence had faded. No, that was the wrong word; "faded" sounded gentle and natural, something that occurred in the ordinary progression of time. In this case I had the feeling that someone had made a concentrated effort at erasure.

There were so many unanswered questions. Who were the couple in the master bedroom? Why had the woman been crying, and what was the dream that her husband seemed to know so well that it did not have to be described? The "Kathy" she had cried out to must have been the "Katherine Abbott" in the high school yearbook, the sweet-faced blonde girl with the wide smile. The room with the riding trophies had to have been Kathy's room. There had been no sense of Lia's presence there. The clothing in the closet, the half-completed homework on the desk, the careless clutter, so natural for the room of a teenager, had all been Kathy's. But where was the girl herself?

And where was Lia? There had been nothing in any part of the house to indicate that a second girl had made her home there. In the yearbook she had been identified as "Lia Abbott," with the same last name as Kathy's. Had Lia been adopted by the Abbott family as I had by the Strattons?

I was jerked from my reverie by the sudden clatter of ice pellets raining against the balcony doors. I pulled myself up on one elbow so that I could see past the balcony to the water. The sea was the color of charcoal, and it was churning as madly as though it were in a pot on a hot burner. For as far as I could see waves were cresting and breaking in long, jagged lines of froth. From my position I did not have a view of the rocks, but I could imagine them, slick and black beneath an icy torrent of rushing water. I pictured our ledge, Jeff's and mine, and shuddered.

My eyes shifted to the clock on the bedside table, and I caught my breath in surprise. It was already well past eight! Could I really have been gone that long? I was beginning to realize that there was no sense of time connected with these astral journeys. If distance could be covered in an instant, it reduced the concept of minutes and hours to unreality. Why hadn't one of the children been sent to wake me?

Or, perhaps one *had!* That thought was enough to bring me upright with a start of panic. What if, as he had so many times before, Neal had come to shake me awake for school, and I had not responded! He would have been terrified!

Scrambling quickly out of bed, I snatched up my robe from where it hung across the back of the desk chair and hurried out into the hallway. The phone was ringing. It jangled twice and then was silent. I started down the stairs, and as I came abreast of the living room I heard voices floating up from the kitchen. Their pitch was ordinary. No one sounded upset or frightened.

I let my breath out slowly in a sigh of relief and continued on down the rest of the way at a more leisurely rate, buttoning my robe as I went.

When I entered the kitchen I found the children, still in their pajamas, seated at the breakfast table, eating French toast.

Mother was standing at the stove, stirring a spoonful of instant coffee into a cup of hot water. She greeted me with a smile.

"Hi, there, honey. Did our hailstorm wake you?"

"There's no school today!" Neal announced jubilantly, and Megan said, "Jeff just called."

"No school," I repeated. "Jeff—" as I tried to get the various items of information into workable order.

"They told it on the radio," Neal said. "It's because of the storm. It's supposed to get worse, and Mr. Ziegler's scared if he takes us across we might get stuck there."

"That makes sense," I acknowledged. "And what about Jeff?"

"I said you were still asleep," Meg said. "He said for you to call him when you woke up."

"Do you want toast?" Mother asked. "No, first, I guess, you'd better return Jeff's call. I can't believe the lines will stay up much longer."

"I'll call him from the other extension," I said.

"Secrets?" Meg asked with sudden interest.

"They wouldn't be if I told you," I said, and went back up the stairs to the living room.

I had my finger poised, ready to dial Jeff's number, when I was struck with the realization that I had nothing to report. I knew what he expected — a full account of my trip to find Lia. What a letdown it would be when I admitted that it had been a failure! Not only had I fallen short of my destination, but I had gleaned no new information of any importance. The only actual discovery had been the name in the yearbook, and that meant nothing unless I could understand its significance.

But, was it true? Had I learned nothing? I had been in Lia's home. I had moved through rooms that she had once occupied. I had seen her adoptive parents and observed the setting within which she must have lived. Surely, I must have absorbed something meaningful!

I forced my mind back, concentrating on detail. The mountains, the clear, dry air, the Indian blanket, the two-hour time difference, all helped to place the Abbotts' home in the Southwest. In what city and state did they live? I had the nagging feeling that I should know. I had seen something and had let it slip by. Had there been lettering on a mailbox? No, I was sure that there hadn't. The license plate on the camper would have helped, but I had paid it no attention.

Mentally, I retraced my passage into the living room and let my mind's eye move slowly about, lighting first one place and then another. I saw again the rich texture of the draperies, the well-filled bookshelves, the television console —

And there, I stopped. On the top of the TV set there had been envelopes. In the top, left corner of each had been written a return address. I focused on it briefly. I had not taken in the name of the street and the house number, but — the town? I squeezed my eyes shut and tried to picture the handwriting. Abruptly, I saw it — saw the whole word spelled out — ALBUQUERQUE. The Abbotts lived in Albuquerque, New Mexico!

So, I did know *something!* And the key to further knowledge lay right at my fingertips. Hesitating only a second, I lifted the receiver and dialed Information.

The operator on the mainland connected me with Directory Assistance in Albuquerque. The faint, far voice asked me the name of the party I wished to reach.

"Abbott," I said, and then recalled the voice of the sleep-dazed woman in the huge bed. "Oh, Art, it was so real!" The name — Art? "It's Arthur," I said. "Arthur Abbott."

I expected that there would be dozens, but luck was with me. There was one Arthur Abbott living on Stagecoach Road.

The operator gave me the number, and I dialed it direct.

The phone rang and rang. It was a woman's voice that finally answered, and I recognized it at once. It was a strange sensation to hear over the telephone wire what I had listened to in person so short a time ago.

"Hello?"

"I'm sorry to be calling this early," I said, realizing that it was likely that my call had awakened her. "I'm trying to get in touch with Lia."

There was a long silence. I began to wonder if we might have been disconnected.

Then the woman asked, "Who is this?"

"My name's Laurie Stratton," I said. "I'm a sort of relative. I've lost touch with Lia, and I'm trying to find her."

"You're related to Lia?" There was disbelief in her voice, and something else as well. I could not pinpoint it exactly, but it sharpened her tone, and the words came at me, clipped and harsh, with spaces between them.

I thought of how Mother had reacted to the idea of my trying to make contact with my natural family. She had felt upset and threatened. If Mrs. Abbott was Lia's adoptive mother, it was not surprising that she might be reacting with identical emotions.

"I don't want to disturb anything," I assured her. "Please, believe me. I'm not interrupting Lia's life. She's the one who got in touch."

There was another strange silence. When Mrs. Abbott spoke again, her voice was flat and expressionless.

"I'll get my husband."

A moment later Mr. Abbott came on the line.

"This is Art Abbott. You're trying to reach Lia?"

"Yes," I told him. "I'm Laurie Stratton, Lia's natural sister. I don't want to cause problems. Lia and I have already communicated. It's just that she never told me where her home was. I've been trying to locate her."

"Lia doesn't have a sister," Mr. Abbott said. "At least, we were never informed about one. Do you know the name of the agency that placed you?"

"Hastings in Gallup," I said. "I was adopted by the Strattons when I was a baby. Lia and I are twins. She remained with her natural mother for a while, and then, I think, she was put up for adoption also. I believe it might have been through the same agency."

"It was." His tone had altered slightly. I could tell that he was beginning to believe me. "You're Lia's twin? Fraternal or identical?"

"Identical," I said.

"Dear God!" It was a moment before he seemed able to continue. When he did, it was in a rush, as though he wanted to get everything said as quickly as possible.

"We didn't adopt Lia. At one point we planned to, but the legal procedures were never completed. She was our foster child for eighteen months. She had been in three homes before ours. None of the placements worked out. We couldn't understand it. She was an attractive girl with a magnetic personality. Our daughter, Kathy, adored her. It seemed incredible to us that her previous families could have rejected her as they did."

"They rejected her?"

"Accidents happen. We can't know why things occur as they do, but, painful or not, we must accept them. At least, that's how we felt then. A foster child deserves the same loyalty you give a natural child. We'd had foster kids before, and they'd added so much to our lives. My wife and I love children. We'd have had a dozen of our own if we'd been able."

"So you took Lia to live with you?" I prodded gently, hoping to get him back onto the original subject.

"We thought it would be great. She could be a sister to Kathy. They were in the same grade, and they got on beautifully. Kathy taught her to ride, and the girls would go off on trail rides together after school and on weekends. We got Lia her own horse. We never played favorites. We were lucky enough to be able to provide well for them, and we wanted them both to have whatever they needed to be happy."

"And was Lia happy?" How odd it seemed to be talking with someone who had lived with Lia and knew her, not just as a vision and a voice, but as a daughter.

"She was, and she wasn't," Mr. Abbott said slowly.

"What do you mean?"

"She liked it here, but at times she seemed depressed. She'd go into her room and lock the door. She said she was sleeping. If she was, it was like the sleep of the dead. We couldn't rouse her for a phone call or dinner or anything. That disturbed us. People don't act that way unless there's something bothering them."

"Did she tell you what it was?"

Mr. Abbott hesitated. Then he said, "She told us —" There was an odd note in his voice. "She told us she was getting too attached to us."

"Too attached? But how could that —"

"She was scared she might lose us. That's what she said, anyway. It had happened before, she said. Every time she'd get settled into a place and start to feel she belonged there, the family would decide they didn't want her. She said she felt she was with us 'on loan.' It was pitiful to see a young girl so insecure. That's why we decided to adopt."

"But it didn't go through?" When he did not respond, I asked another question. "Where is Lia now?"

"Let me ask you something," Mr. Abbott said. "Is your life happy? Are your parents good people?"

"Great people," I said.

"Then stop this search. Let Lia be. She's nothing to you except for the fact that one woman gave birth to you."

"It's not that simple," I said. "It's gone too far. I don't expect you to understand, but I have to find her."

"Well, it won't be here," Mr. Abbott said. "She's no longer with us. She's in a hospital."

"In a hospital!" I exclaimed. "You mean, she's sick?"

"She's sick, and she's not going to get better. If you came here, you couldn't see her. She's not allowed visitors. My advice to you, Miss Stratton, is to concentrate on your own life —"

There was a crackling sound, and the line went dead.

For a long time I stood, unmoving, holding the silent receiver against my ear. How was it possible that I could have come so close to the knowledge I was seeking, only to have it slip so suddenly through my fingers! Mother had warned me. We all of us knew what storms could do. There were periods every winter when we were isolated for hours and sometimes even days. But, why, I asked myself, did it have to happen *now?* In one moment I could have asked Arthur Abbott the name and location of Lia's hospital!

Was that information necessary? Was it possible that I could reach Lia without it? I did not know. The projection experience was so new to me that I was not certain how much control I actually had. I had been able to travel to Helen at will, but I had known precisely where she was to be found. My second attempt had been less successful. Was that because I had not directed myself toward an exact geographical location? Or was it because fear had diverted me? I had known there was no danger connected with my visit to Helen.

Lia had told me that our mother had searched the state of California for our father. She had found him, or so Lia supposed. And Lia, herself, had managed to locate *me*. Had she had leads to go on? If so, what?

I did have some idea of where I should be looking. "Even if you came here," Mr. Abbott had told me, "you couldn't see her." He had not said "if you *went there*," but "if you *came here*." Lia was in a hospital somewhere in the vicinity of Albuquerque. And I no longer would have my fear of her as a deterrent. Lia was no threat if she was as ill as her foster father had indicated.

What illness could it be that had come upon her so violently and quickly? To me, she had seemed invincible. The thought of her in a hospital bed was almost impossible to contemplate.

"But, she is human," I reminded myself, speaking the words aloud in an effort to make them more convincing. "Somewhere she exists as a real person, subject to viruses and infections like the rest of us. But for him to say that she will never get better —"

How could that be? Had she been in an accident? Had she been stricken with some progressive disease? Surprisingly, this conjecture brought me no pleasure. It was a relief to feel unthreatened, and there should have been satisfaction in the thought that one who sought to injure others would receive punishment.

At the same time —

We are the two sides of a coin. We floated together in the same sea before birth.

Despite everything, the fact remained that Lia was my sister.

CHAPTER 19

MY SISTER.

If the other elements had not been there — if I had not had some idea of where to search — if I had not become, in some strange way, so close to her — still, I would have found her. I am as sure of that as I have ever been of anything. We were identical sisters, drawn together by a force that transcended logic.

"She's nothing to you," Mr. Abbott had said, "except for the fact that one woman gave birth to you."

That was true. But, it was enough.

It could not be done at once. Megan was already shouting up the stairs that my French toast was getting cold. I entered the kitchen, and as though that were a signal, the electricity went off.

That was the catalyst that always triggered Mother's decision to clean out drawers. It made sense, actually, because during normal times she and Dad were too occupied to think about such things, but when light was gone and the electric typewriter could not operate, they were left with all this creative energy and nothing to focus it on. So she got my father out of bed, and we all took candles and flashlights and shoveled out drawers in the kitchen and the bathrooms. It was not dull work. We are a family that does not throw things away. The drawers contained a multitude of notes recalling earlier times — "Gone to Kimmie's — be back by 5"; "Agent called — Finnigan wants film option on 'Lord of the Stars' "; "Defrost hamburger!" There were receipts and corks and empty toothpaste tubes and newspaper clippings. We filled two trash bags, and then Dad decided we had worked long enough, so he built a fire in the living room fireplace and suggested we tell stories.

Of course, he went first, and it was really a form of cheating because what he told was a book plot he was mulling over and wanted to try out on us. When he was done, Meg took the floor and gave us a tale about a day when the sun blew out and the world grew colder and colder until our whole family crammed into the bathtub and turned on the hot water.

"And then that froze," she continued, "and we were trapped there in the ice, and we starved to death because the box of cookies we had brought in with us was up on top of the sink."

Neal's story was about dragons, and it never went anywhere because he got so wrapped up in their physical description that he forgot to have them do anything.

The turn passed to me. I told a story about twin sisters who were separated at birth and who found each other because one of them knew a secret. She could lift herself from her body and fly.

"And she crossed the land," I said, "and found her twin, in the far place where she lived, and she started by visiting her at night, so at first the other sister thought the whole thing was a dream. But then the visiting twin grew stronger in the use of her talent, and she was able to appear in the daylight. And she told her sister, 'You can do this also, if you try. And you *must* try. You must learn, so that you will be able to travel the way I do, with the speed of thought, leaving your body behind.'"

Everyone was silent when I had finished. Then Neal said, "You make it sound almost like it's true. It isn't, is it? People can't do that?"

"No, people can't do that," Mother said decidedly. She turned to me accusingly. "You just can't let it drop, can you, Laurie? You've got to keep throwing it back at us. And what an unfair way to do it, in the guise of fun!"

"Now, Shelly," Dad said, "I'm sure Laurie didn't mean it that way."

"Yes, she did," Mother insisted. "It's the same awful story she tried to tell us that first day about visitations and dreams and spirits coming and going. She's obsessed with the idea of locating her roots."

"What roots?" Neal asked, his eyes brightening with interest. "Like the show on television?"

"Now, see!" Mother said. "You've brought the children into it."

"I'm sorry," I said, and meant it. I had not imagined that the story would upset her to this degree. "I'm not trying to 'throw' anything back at you. I swear it. Astral projection is a fact, Mother, and people from my sort of background are particularly adept at using it. I have books on the subject that you can read if you'd like to. And this morning I made a phone call —"

"Please, drop it," Dad said quietly. "You know how your mother feels about the idea of digging up the past. Putting it into a fictional context doesn't make it any more palatable to her. She's right; it's an unfair maneuver, and I can't see what you think there is to gain by it. We've already given you all the information we have."

"What if I told you it was true?" I said. "What if I could prove to you that Lia had really taught me —"

"That's enough, Laurie," Dad said emphatically. "Your turn is over. It's come round to you, Shelly. What's your story to be about?"

"I can't think of one," Mother said in a strained voice. "We've spent enough time on this. How about lunch? Neal, bring the flashlight. The bulb won't go on when we open the refrigerator, you know. It will be like playing 'Go Fish' to find makings for sandwiches."

They would never believe me. The realization struck me with a kind of hopeless finality. Their creativity — the very thing that might have been supposed to have made them receptive — was what closed them off. My parents were used to building worlds for other people, and they fashioned these like expert craftsmen, conscious always that what they were creating was not to be confused with reality. Stories were fiction — Meg's frozen bath water, Neal's platoon of dragons. I was breaking the rules if I took the game beyond that and insisted that the incredible might be true.

Suddenly I wanted Jeff. He was the only one I could talk to, and I wanted him so desperately that I was tempted to rush out and brave the storm.

"I'm not hungry," I told my parents. "I'll get something later. I'm going upstairs to read for a while."

I was halfway to the landing when I heard footsteps behind me.

"Laurie?" Megan asked. "Is 'Lia' the name of the ghosty?"

I turned. The round face, raised to mine, was solemn and worried, and the pale brows were drawn together in a frown.

"You believe me, Meg?" I asked her.

"Yes," Megan said. "What I don't understand, though, is why she wanted so much for you to learn how to go away."

'Why, because — because —" To my surprise, I found that I was unable to come up with an answer. I had accepted Lia's insistence without questioning it. "Try again, Laurie," she had kept telling me. "Tired or not, you must keep trying." Why had it mattered to her so much? I had not known then, and I did not know now.

"It scares me," Meg said.

"She can't hurt me, honey." I took three quick steps down the stairs and put my arms around her, pulling her sturdy body against me in a hard hug. "She's far away and very sick. The part of her that comes here is just the thinking part. She can't hurt people with that. It's like — well, like a shadow maybe. A shadow can't do anything, can it?"

"I guess not," Meg said, but she sounded unconvinced. "You be careful, okay?"

"Of course I will." That tone of reassurance, I can hear it now, ringing out confidently in that darkened hall. And beyond my voice, the sound of the wind, and beyond that —

Was there another sound? Muffled, as though a hand had been pressed quickly over unseen lips? Was it laughter?

Did Megan hear it? Was that the reason she clung to me so tightly for that extra moment after my own arms had released their hold?

215

"You be careful," she said again before she left me, and, again, I assured her that I would be.

I climbed the rest of the stairs and went down the hall to my room. The wind was louder here, and the glass of the balcony doors was so plastered with snow that I had the disconcerting feeling that I was sealed off from the world. Even so, I pulled shut the bedroom door and then reached automatically for the light switch. It made an ineffectual clicking sound, and the room seemed to grow even darker.

I groped my way across to the unmade bed and stretched myself out on top of the rumpled blankets.

"I'm coming to find you, sister," I whispered to Lia.

The safe time, Jeff and I had decided, was the morning, but did that matter now? As I'd said to Megan, there was nothing Lia could do to hurt me. Just as her shadow could cause no harm to my body, there was no way that her body could cause injury to my spirit self. I was wise to her. She could not fool me with illusions. She could not entice me into a disaster situation as she had Jeff and Helen. I knew too much about her. I would not allow myself to be drawn into danger.

Laughter?

No, it was the wind. It was water rushing across the rocks beneath the window. It was the whisper of snow piling layer on layer on the slanted roof of Cliff House.

I closed my eyes and put my mind into focus. And like an arrow snapped from a bow, I went.

It was all so fast I had no chance to weigh what was happening. There was no entrance to make — I was simply *there*. The place was a hospital, but it was not the same as the one in which Helen had been. At first I could not ascertain where the difference lay. There were the same white walls, the same sterile atmosphere with the immaculate waxed surfaces of linoleum floors reflecting the glow of the fluorescent lights on the ceilings. Nurses and orderlies moved efficiently through the halls, carrying charts and hypodermics and wheeling trays of medications.

But there were no flowers, and that was surprising. At Duke the front desk had been loaded with them — baskets of blooms, vases of cut arrangements, potted plants — all tagged and awaiting delivery to patients.

Here there were none. The desk was bare. And the doors to the patients' rooms were closed.

I moved slowly down the hall. Nurses passed me or walked straight through me, unaware of my existence. I no longer found this startling; it was what I expected. The doors were strange in that the upper portions of them were made of glass. I could look through and see the people in the rooms beyond, standing, sitting, staring out of the windows or at the walls or moving restlessly about. No one seemed ill in any serious way.

"— she's sick — she's not allowed visitors —"

Mr. Abbott's words came back to me, and I found it hard to make sense out of them. The people on this ward did not appear to be sick enough to warrant such a rule. Yet he was right. There were no visitors, and it was a time of day when there should have been.

I passed one door after another until I came to the one I was seeking. I did not have to look through the glass to know whose room it was. It was as though a voice were calling out to me.

I passed through the door and moved across to the bed and stood beside it, gazing down in wonder at the familiar figure.

She was a duplicate of myself.

She was sleeping so soundly that it hardly seemed possible that she was alive. Her chest did not appear to be moving, and there was no quiver of eyelids or nostrils. I bent closer to examine the contours of the face. The starkly defined bone structure, the olive complexion, the thick fringe of lashes lying motionless against the smooth cheek might well have been my own.

Yet there were differences.

This girl's ears were pierced, and mine were not. Mother and I had gone through a few rounds on that issue, and she had won. "There are enough natural holes in a person's anatomy," she had said firmly, "so that it's a sacrilege to make new ones unless you absolutely have to." I didn't agree, but it hadn't seemed worth waging an all-out battle. It would be easy enough to get the job done when I went off to college.

There was a tiny scar on the chin that might have been nothing more than the result of scratching an insect bite, but it was a scar that I did not have.

There was a mole on the neck at a spot where I had no mole.

I continued my inspection. The girl lay on her side with her knees drawn up against her stomach. She was covered with a blanket, and one hand was curled around its edge. She had perfect fingernails, the kind that had always filled me with envy. My own had a scraggly look, not exactly "bitten to the quick," but "slightly gnawed."

Small things. Unimportant. Almost unnoticeable, yet they spelled the difference between Lia Abbott and Laurie Stratton. This body was not mine, and the girl who dwelt in

218

it was someone else. Her genetic makeup might be identical, but she had lived a different life and made her own marks upon the body's surface.

"Lia?" I spoke the name, but no sound came.

Could she hear me, I wondered? *I* had heard *her* when I was sleeping. Her voice had become a part of my dreaming and as it had grown stronger had expanded into my waking consciousness.

"Lia?" I said again.

Behind me there was a tiny, metallic sound. The door swung open, and a nurse came into the room. She crossed to the foot of the bed and stood there a moment, staring down at the figure of the sleeping girl. Then she turned and left. She pulled the door closed and paused on its far side to glance back through the glass.

There was another sharp click, as though a key were being turned in a lock. Was it possible, I asked myself incredulously, that they were *locking Lia in?*

I could not test the door, but I could move through it out into the corridor beyond. It was true. The nurse was holding a ring of keys. She went back to the desk and handed them to another uniformed woman who placed them in a drawer.

"So, how's our little wildcat?" the second woman asked.

"Sound asleep. I don't know why you call her that. I've never seen her move a muscle. It's almost like she was in a coma."

"You're on swing shift." The woman at the desk was obviously the older of the two. A network of fine lines branched out from the corners of her eyes, and her short hair was a pepper-and-salt mixture of black and gray. "I was on duty the morning they brought her in. You should have seen her then! They had to use a straitjacket. This sleeping thing makes me nervous. It's just not natural."

"It's afternoon siesta time," the younger nurse said lightly. "I wish they were all this accommodating, especially the old gal down in 512 who does all that yelling."

"I'm serious. This doesn't fit any pattern I've seen before. The ones who go comatose tend to stay that way. This one's alert in the mornings. She has the session with her doctor and goes from there to occupational therapy. You'd swear she was as normal as apple pie if you didn't know better."

"That doesn't sound like any wildcat."

"No, she sits on that. Keeps it tucked down under. Then, suddenly — wham! All hell breaks loose. And then — zonk — she's asleep again. Like a dead thing. Have you ever tried to wake her when she's out like that?"

"No way! I believe in letting well enough alone. When they're sleeping they can't give us any trouble." The younger woman paused. "She's such a pretty kid, so sort of sweet looking. It's hard to imagine her doing something all that terrible."

"And she's so young, too — only seventeen. If they'd been able to try her as an adult, I bet she'd be in the State Pen instead of here. 'Innocent by reason of insanity!' That was a copout decision, if you ask me. It got them off the hook as far as not having to stick her in a detention home. They couldn't take that risk. You don't put a piranha in with a bowlful of goldfish."

"Do you really think she's that dangerous?"

"Let's put it this way — I sure wouldn't want her moving in with *me*." The older nurse shook her head. "That poor Katherine Abbott. It said in the paper that she landed with the horse *on top of her*. It's a wonder she lived long enough to tell what happened."

"Lia forced her off the cliff?"

"That's what Katherine said before she died. She said the girl came riding right at her, waving her sweater in the air and screaming like a banshee. The Abbott girl was riding a high-strung show horse. It started rearing and — this is what the paper said, but it's never made much sense to me — Lia pulled her own horse to a stop right before it reached them, but Lia herself, she just seemed to *keep on coming.*"

"That's crazy," the young nurse said. "You mean, she was thrown forward?"

"She must have meant that, although the way the newspaper had it, it didn't sound that way. The way Katherine was quoted, she saw one girl slumped over in the saddle and another zooming at her through the air. And then she was falling."

"That must have been a misprint."

"Or the girl was hallucinating. Either way, Lia rode on home just like nothing had happened. She told Mrs. Abbott that Katherine had decided to stay out longer and ride up to one of the higher pastures. When she wasn't back by dinnertime, her father took Lia's horse and went out looking for her. He's the one who found her."

"The poor man!" The young nurse shuddered. "You said the horse was on top of her?"

"And the girl was still conscious! It was one of those one-in-a-million possibilities. The hoofprints on the trail substantiated her story. There were other things, really weird ones, that kept coming out at the trial, though the judge called them immaterial. There had been other families she'd lived with where people had had accidents. In one of them a baby, an only child, had suffocated in its crib, and in another a little boy —"

I could listen no longer.

The pieces were coming together. The picture was not complete yet, but the horrible outline was there in its entirety. This was a mental institution, and the girl on the bed — my sister, Lia — was an inmate. A physical inmate only, because her spirit self could not be imprisoned. In the mornings she dutifully saw her doctor and participated in whatever scheduled activities were prescribed for her, but in the afternoons and evenings —

"— it's almost like she was in a coma. . . . Have you ever tried to wake her when she's out like that?"

No, of course they could not wake her. She was not sleeping. She was *gone!*

The body in the room I had visited was an empty envelope. Lia, the real Lia, was elsewhere. Perhaps even now, at this very moment, she was on Brighton Island, walking the dunes. Perhaps she stood on the rocks outside of Cliff House, gazing out across the wild beauty of the churning ocean. Or perhaps she had entered Cliff House. Entered? *Invaded!* What right did she have to come into my home uninvited? According to what I had just overheard, she had managed to mess up her own life in a horrible way. God alone knew what could have driven her to do what she had done, but that was no concern of mine. I was not responsible for Lia. My life was my own. And it revolved around my real family — the parents who had raised me — my brother, Neal — my sister, Megan —

Megan!

At the thought of Meg a sudden chill shot through me.

Until today I had not realized quite how perceptive my small sister was. Not only had she accepted the concept of astral projection, she had identified Lia as the "ghosty" whose presence haunted our home.

Was Meg a threat to Lia? Could she possibly be considered one? It was hard to imagine someone with Lia's powers feeling threatened by an eight-year-old. What could Meg do to her? What could anyone do, for that matter? Surely, Lia had nothing to fear from any of us.

Yet, the fact remained that the only two other people who had shared my knowledge about Lia had met with near-fatal accidents. And Kathy Abbott — what of her! Lia was dangerous, more dangerous than I had ever imagined! And if she was indeed insane, how could I expect her attacks to be based on reason?

She mustn't hurt Megan!

The words were a silent scream within me. The cord snapped tight, and back I flew to Cliff House!

As soon as the familiar walls were around me, I realized that my panic had been unfounded. The family was gathered safely in the living room, munching on peanut butter sandwiches and playing a word game. Mother had settled back to normal. She was even laughing a little at some silly pun that Dad had made. Neal was preparing to put another log on the fire, and Meg herself was authoritatively explaining that "just because you put an *s* at the end of a word, it doesn't make it a different word. It's just more of the same word it was before, so it shouldn't count."

My love for them rose within me with such force that it was painful. This was where I belonged, let Lia drift where she chose. I knew enough about her now to be able to protect myself and the people I cared about. Jeff and I would hash things over later and try to put my new discoveries into perspective. For now I simply wanted to join my family.

In my room the body of a slender, dark-haired girl lay as I had left it. I moved toward it, anticipating the instant when the astral cord would whip me into possession. To my surprise, that moment did not come. Instead, I felt a resistance, as though someone had constructed an invisible barrier. I knew this was impossible. If there was one thing the books that Helen had bought for me were adamant about it was that the strength of the cord increased as the spirit self approached its physical counterpart. How could this magnetic field suddenly have reversed itself?

There was no way that the cord could be broken except by death, and my body was not dead. It was just in a state of suspended animation.

As though to give proof to this the girl on the bed opened her eyes.

I stared at her, incredulous. Those were my eyes! How could they open unless I willed them to? This was my face — my body! This was *myself!*

The girl sat up and yawned and stretched her arms above her sleep-tousled head.

"I guess I'm hungry after all," she said.

CHAPTER 20

THE HOURS THAT FOLLOWED HAVE MELDED in my mind into a blur. I've heard that the mind does that in times of total horror to protect itself from snapping. The girl from the bedroom — (What shall I call her? Laurie? No — for *I* was Laurie — I have always been Laurie!) — that girl went to the kitchen and made herself a sandwich. I watched, helpless, as Laurie's hands — *my* hands — spread peanut butter onto a slice of bread and placed another slice over it. I watched as she carried her lunch back up to the living room and sat down with my parents and the children in front of the fireplace.

Numb with shock, impotent to do anything to stop her, I heard Lia speaking with Laurie's voice.

"Hi," she said.

"Hi, dear," Mother answered. "Look, I'm sorry about the way I jumped all over you earlier. Dad thinks I overreacted, and he's probably right."

"That's all right," the girl said. "It didn't bother me."

"Of course it did, or you wouldn't have run off like that."

"It's like beating a dead horse," Dad said. "The subject is one that is not going to get us anywhere. Your mother does overreact to it, but that's not her fault. Talking about it or hearing you talk about it upsets her. There's no sense in continuing to do it. Okay?"

"Okay," Lia said. "I'm sorry. Why should I be worrying over a past I can't remember? Isn't it enough that I now live at Cliff House?"

"I wish you'd talk sense," Neal complained. "First it's that stuff about 'roots,' and now it's this. What was it that Mother got so mad about? What 'past' can't you remember?"

"Her babyhood," Dad said smoothly. "Can you recall yours?"

"Not all the way," Neal said. "I can remember when you and Mother brought Meg home from the hospital. She had a real scrunched-up face and no teeth."

"I think I was cute," Meg observed placidly. "I've seen the pictures in the album. The earliest thing I can remember is my christening. I was wearing this beautiful white dress with lace all over it, and they put water on my forehead."

"You can't remember that," Neal objected. "You were much too little. People's brains don't start recording things until they're at least a couple of years old, do they, Dad?"

"I don't know about that," Dad said. "The memories are there, but the retrieval process is a different thing entirely—"

And they were off again on one of those discussions that the members of my family delight in.

Lia sat quiet, eating her sandwich and listening. The firelight flickered across her face, throwing shadows into the hollows of her cheeks and accentuating the tilt of her alien eyes. It was a strange sensation to watch this face — *my* face — in a light in which I had never seen it. I had never thought of my face as pretty. I still did not, but I could see a certain quality, a haunting strangeness, that might have accounted for Gordon's attraction. The coloring, the features, held a touch of something that was not quite Mary Beth Ziegler, not quite Natalie Coleson.

Lia shifted her position and settled back against Dad's knee, and one of his hands dropped casually to rest on her hair. She looked so comfortable there, so much a natural part of this close-knit group. She was not an intruder. She was Laurie Stratton.

And if *she* was Laurie Stratton — then, who was I?

What was that silly game show that Neal found so intriguing, the one where people challenged each other's identities? I couldn't recall the name of it, only the punch line:

"Will the *real* John Jones" (or "Mary Smith" or whatever the name might be) "please stand up?"

"I knew it!" Neal would announce with satisfaction. "I always guess them right."

So what had happened to that amazing ability? Couldn't he tell his own sister from an imposter? "Will the real Laurie Stratton please stand up?" Neal didn't ask it, and neither did the others. They had their Laurie in the shape and form they were used to. Unseen, unsensed, my spirit self did not exist for them.

"Be careful," Meg had warned me.

"I will," I had assured her.

It had been an easy promise to make. And to break. What, after all, was "careful"? I would be careful not to go out on the rocks again. I would take the greatest care not to dash off down icy trails as Helen had. But, aside from these precautions, how was one "careful" of a being without substance? "A shadow can't do anything," I had told Megan, so surely, so smugly. I had been right. A shadow could do nothing, unless it ceased to be a shadow. Unless it managed to claim a body left vacated and unguarded by someone stupid enough to believe herself invulnerable.

The day moved on. At some point along the way, the sound of the wind began to lessen and the house grew oddly still.

"It's turning," said Mother.

I knew that by morning if this followed the pattern of most winter storms, the sun would be peering through holes in the ragged clouds and the sky would be patched with segments of blue. The beaches would be crusted with ice, and the carcasses of frozen fish would line the shore. By midday, boats from the mainland would have made the crossing, and phone lines would be up, and we would have electricity. Mother would be painting, and Dad's typewriter would be pounding away to make up for all these wasted hours.

When dinnertime came, five people gathered in the kitchen to eat a cold supper by candlelight. Dad poured extra wine, and he and Mother became talkative, laughing a bit more than usual and reminiscing.

"Remember the storm that grounded that baby whale on the beach? They had to send the Coast Guard to tow it away."

"Remember the one that brought in a million starfish?"

"What I remember best," Mother said, "is all those years when we used to dream about what it would be like to live on an island. We'd ride around New York Harbor on the ferry with people shoved up against us on all sides, and we'd pretend we were on our way to some private place where there would be nothing but surf and wind and sunshine."

"And one day you really got here," Neal said.

"Yes, one day we did. I wonder how many people have a dream as big as that one and actually see it come true?"

"Not many," Dad said. "We were lucky. We worked hard, sure, but our work got put in front of the right people at the right time."

"Sometimes I feel almost guilty," Mother said, "about having so much when there are other people with so little. I don't mean just having Cliff House, but careers we enjoy and each other and healthy, beautiful kids and so few problems. That day when Laurie and I went to the hospital after Helen's accident, I kept thinking, dear Lord, what if this had happened to one of ours! It's like there was some sort of lucky star shining over us. When Laurie took that awful fall between the rocks, she was hardly even hurt. It was poor Jeff who had a leg broken."

" 'Poor Jeff' is right," Dad said. "That kid's had his share. What's the deal with that face of his, Laurie? Can't they do anything about it? Plastic surgery can correct a lot of things. I read in *Newsweek* the other day about a girl who had her whole face destroyed in an auto accident, and they're building it back for her."

"I don't know," Lia said without much interest. "Maybe his father can't afford it."

"Can't afford it!" Dad exclaimed. "Pete Rankin may not live high, but that waterfront property of his has tripled in value since he bought it."

"His lady friend won't let him sell," Meg said.

Mother turned to her in astonishment.

"Where in the world did you hear that?"

"From Mrs. DeWitt. She cleans Tuesdays for Mrs. Briggs. She heard her talking on the phone to her sister on the mainland who goes to the same beauty parlor as Mr. Rankin's lady friend."

"You pick up information like a vacuum cleaner," Mother said. "Is there anything you don't know about anybody?"

"I don't know why Laurie's eating white meat," said Meg.

There was a moment's silence. The girl at the end of the table paused with her fork halfway to her mouth. Then she lowered it and laid it on her plate. In the dim light of the dancing candle flames, I could not read the expression in her eyes, but when she spoke her voice was strained.

"Is there a law that says I have to eat dark meat?"

"No," Meg said, "but you always do."

"People's tastes can change."

"I'm glad if you don't like drumsticks anymore," Neal said. "Can I have the second one since Laurie doesn't want it?"

"Finish your salad first." Mother turned back to Dad. "On the subject of laws, isn't there one that says parents have to take care of their children, even if it means selling their investments?"

"They have to support them," Dad said, "but I don't imagine cosmetic surgery comes under that heading. Besides, the boy's too old to be classed as a dependent. What age is he, Laurie? Eighteen? Nineteen, maybe?"

"I don't know."

"You do too know," said Megan. "He'll be nineteen in April. You told me that last week."

Lia's face remained expressionless, but I felt something coil behind it, a whip of fury aimed at Megan, like a snake drawn back to strike. Now it was my turn to cry, *Be careful! Take care; oh, please, take care! You don't know what danger you're in!*

Meg could not have heard me, but she did fall silent.

Our parents were still on the subject of the Rankins.

"If Jeff's over eighteen, I don't think Pete can be forced to do anything," Dad was saying. "At the same time, why should any father have to be forced on a thing like that? What sort of priorities does that guy have? Your kid is your kid, no matter what age he is. That boy's face should be more important than some woman. I don't know what plastic surgery would run to, but I can't imagine that there wouldn't be some way —"

Lia was no longer eating. She was simply sitting there, gazing at Megan. Meg was chewing on a chicken wing. She seemed to be trying to sort something out in her mind. After a moment she raised her own eyes to meet Lia's. She said nothing. She just kept gnawing away at that bone, while our parents' conversation continued on the far side of the table.

Neal said, "I'm done with my salad."

"No, you're not," Mother told him without looking. "You've hidden it under your bread crusts."

She knew us so well! Mother's life was her art and her family. How could she miss the fact that one of the children at this table was not her own!

"May I be excused?" Meg asked.

"Sure," Dad said. "If you're finished."

"I think I'll go to bed."

That captured Mother's immediate attention.

"So early, honey? Aren't you feeling well?"

"I'm not exactly sick," Meg said.

"Is something else the matter?"

"I don't know. It's like — something's funny. I don't know what it is. I just feel like I don't want to stay down here anymore."

"It's been a funny sort of day," Dad agreed. "Everything's been off-kilter. I think we'll all be better off turning in early. There's not much you can do at night without electricity."

Meg got up from the table and went around to kiss our parents goodnight. Mother gave her a flashlight to carry, and she went upstairs. I accompanied her. She paused at the open door of her and Neal's bedroom, and then, as though following a sudden impulse, she continued up the stairs to my room. She entered it and did not seem to know what to do next. Slowly she let the beam of the flashlight circle the room, playing it in an uncertain manner over the walls and furniture. Then she switched off the light and crossed to stand at the balcony doors.

It had stopped snowing, and the sky had cleared enough now so that a few stars could be seen, trembling against the dark like far, pale fireflies. Megan watched them awhile. Then she sighed.

"Something's funny," she said again, softly. Then she clicked the flash on and went back down to her room.

I watched as she put on her nightclothes and stayed beside her until she fell asleep. I would have liked to have been able to feel that I was guarding her, but I knew that my presence was meaningless. In my spirit state, I was helpless to protect her from anything. I wanted desperately to touch her, to feel the soft, light hair beneath my fingers, to encircle the warm, chunky body with my arms, but to Meg that would have been no more reassurance than a slight stir of air in a drafty room.

She tossed restlessly in her bed for a long time and had just dozed off when Neal came in. I watched until he was in his pajamas and had settled himself beneath the covers. It was easier, somehow, to leave them together than to leave Megan alone.

Be careful! Meg, be careful!

I could shriek my warning forever, and to what end? If Meg did sense its meaning, she would not know what precautions to take. The enemy was no longer a stranger but dwelt behind a beloved face.

I moved up the stairway to my own room. Lia was seated on the bed, brushing her hair. The room was dark, and the movement of the brush created tiny sparks of electricity like phosphoresce on a breaking wave in the night sea.

I came to stand beside her. She sensed my presence, and all attempt at pretense fell away.

"Hello," said Lia. "I've been waiting. What took you so long?" I could not have responded if I had been able, for she immediately continued, "Don't bother to answer. I wouldn't be able to hear you. I can't see you either. That visual image your brother saw on the rocks was energized by shock. You haven't enough practice to be able to achieve that at will. I know you're here because I can feel the cord tugging, trying to draw you in. But there is no space. You cannot enter a body that is already occupied."

She lowered the brush, and the sparks ceased. The

darkness could not conceal her face from me. She was smiling.

"Remember the first time you saw me? You were sitting here, as I am now, brushing your hair. This same hair, with this same brush. You saw what you thought was a reflection. Then, slowly, you began to realize that it wasn't. What you didn't know — couldn't know — was that I had been here many times before.

"Back when I was a child our mother told me the name of the people who had adopted you. I never thought much about it. I took it for granted that your life was not much different from my own. After Mother was gone, though, I started wondering about you. I wasn't adopted the way you were. The foster families who took me in had children of their own. Those were the ones they cared about, the ones who would inherit. If those kids hadn't existed, I might have stood a chance.

"The Abbotts were my one real hope. They had money, and they were willing to adopt me. The problem was that they had Kathy. She would always have come first with them, even if they made me legally their daughter. If things had gone as I planned, I would have been their only heir."

The smile was gone now. Her voice was thick with bitterness.

"She lived long enough to turn them all against me. The lawyer the state assigned me was worse than nobody. He told me that if we submitted a plea of insanity I'd get off free. Free! That's a laugh! They shut me up in a bin full of loonies. That's when I decided to find you. I knew where you were. Kathy had brought home a book from the library one day by a writer named James Stratton. There was a picture of him with his family on the back of the jacket, and the biography said they lived on an island off the New England coast. I recognized the name, and the black-haired girl in the photo looked exactly like me. It had to be you! You had it all! And I had nothing!

"Then I came and saw it — the island, the house, your parents! And I knew I would do anything to be in your place."

So you became Laurie. And I? Then, who am I?

She did not need to hear the question.

"You have no more substance than the wind. And you will become even less as time goes by. The force of the mind is drawn from the brain. To keep it alive, you must retain physical contact. Think of a flashlight operating on battery power. If the batteries are not recharged, what eventually will happen?"

She got up from the bed and laid the brush back on the bureau top. Then she turned and began to fold back the bedclothes. There was a gentle, thumping sound as she plumped up the pillow.

"Good night, Laurie," Lia said softly. "Good night — and good-bye."

CHAPTER 21

LIA MADE NO FURTHER ATTEMPT AT COM-munication. It seemed that as far as she was concerned, that formal farewell was to be her last acknowledgment of my existence. The explanation for her actions had been given without apology. To her way of thinking, a wrong had now been righted; an injustice remedied. Whatever obligation she might have felt to prepare me for the inevitable had been fulfilled, and she was through with me.

Lia had what she wanted. I was free to go. But, to go where?

To *die?* She had not offered me that option. I was not to be allowed to move, soul intact, into that natural realm of ultimate projection. Instead, I was to fade, to whisper away, until —

I could not complete the sentence. Until *what?* Was the process endless?

I closed my mind. I could not begin to handle so immense a concept. Instead, I grasped frantically for alternatives. Lia's body lay vacated. I could go and claim it. But what sort of life sentence would I be claiming along with it? To live out Lia's years for her in an institution was hardly less awful than to have no physical identity at all.

Perhaps I could travel. All I needed to do was to think myself someplace, and I would be there. I, who had never known anything other than New England, could now explore the world.

Nor was I confined by the earth! Ingo Swann had been to Mercury! A chapter in the red-covered book had detailed his journey. On his return he had reported that the planet had both an atmosphere and a magnetic field. Astrophysicists and astronomers had declared this impossible, but a short time later the NASA spacecraft, *Mariner* 10, had provided data to confirm Swann's observations.

The idea of astral space travel had excited Jeff tremendously.

"If you can get a grip on this thing, you'll be able to explore the universe!" he had exclaimed.

"No way," I told him emphatically. "I'm not that much of an adventurer."

I had meant it, or thought I meant it, when I said it. Now, however, things were different. I had nothing to lose that I had not lost already. Why shouldn't I, in whatever time of consciousness was left to me, experience the impossible?

Because — because —

Because I couldn't. It was that simple. The people I loved were here on Brighton Island.

And so I stayed. In the days that followed, I grew to know my family well. I spent many mornings in Mother's studio, watching the thin, clever fingers manipulate the brush as she layered colors upon a canvas. The painting was of a windswept beach, and the sky above it was alive with gulls. Their gray wings formed a pattern of arches against the deeper gray of the winter sky. The picture had a haunting quality that held me so that I could not look away. Was the painting really so unique? Or was my reaction due to the fact that this might be the last of her paintings that I would see?

At night, after the rest of the family had gone to bed, I stood at my father's shoulder as he was writing. I listened as he mumbled aloud to himself, trying out lines of dialogue.

" 'What is this world that man would choose to live here? Is it, in truth, so beautiful that he would turn his back upon the stars?' "

Yes, I answered silently. *Yes — yes, it is.*

The ones I spent the most time with were the children. I followed them into the village for the mail and to the homes of their friends and to the landing to board the ferry for school. The boat was back in operation two days after the storm was over, and Meg and Neal, in parkas and boots, clumped their way every day down snow-covered Beach Road, teasing and shoving each other and sliding with shrieks of delight across wide patches of blue-black ice.

Lia walked a bit behind them, unsure about the snow. It must have been the first she had experienced, for she dipped her boots and then lifted them quickly, like a cat. I could almost see the pads of her feet draw up behind the claws.

When Neal, in a moment of eleven-year-old exuberance, tossed a snowball in her direction, she gave a scream and threw up her arms to shield her face.

"Laurie's a sissy!" he yelled, starting to run in premature reaction to the retaliation he expected.

"You brat!" She breathed the words, but Megan, who had fallen back to form a snowball of her own, heard.

She stood, molding the ball with her mittened hands, her eyes on Lia.

238

"You're funny," she said.

"What do you mean by that?" Lia asked sharply.

"You don't act the same as you used to."

"What am I supposed to do, let that brother of yours smash my face in?"

"The snow wasn't hardpacked." She paused, frowning. Megan was frowning a lot these days. *Megan, be careful!* "He's your brother too. Why do you call him *my* brother?"

"Because you're two of a kind, both spoiled rotten. Is there anything you've ever wanted that you haven't been given? Why should you be so much luckier than other people?"

"That's what Mother was saying the other night." Meg tossed the snowball lightly from one hand to the other as she spoke. "Then they got talking about Jeff. Do you know what they're going to do?"

"What?" Lia asked without interest, beginning to walk again.

"They're going to get Jeff's face fixed."

"They're going to do *what?*" Lia stopped dead in her tracks. Shock wiped her face clear of expression. "You just said that to upset me, didn't you?" she said accusingly.

"To upset you?" Meg repeated in surprise. "I thought it would make you happy."

"Well, it doesn't!" Lia's voice was shaking with the effort it took to suppress her fury. "Plastic surgery to repair a mess like that would cost a fortune. People don't throw that kind of money away on strangers!"

"Jeff's not a stranger," Meg said. "He's your boyfriend."

"He most certainly is not. That's been over for a week now. Gordon and I are seeing each other again. We've got dates for both nights this coming weekend. I'd die before I'd be seen in public with a freak like Jeff Rankin."

"That's not how you used to feel."

"It's how I feel *now*," Lia said shortly. "How do you know your parents are planning to do this?"

"They're *our* parents, not just *my* parents."

"Stop talking back and answer my question." Lia's eyes had narrowed to slits. "How do you know it? Did they tell you?"

"No, I heard them talking last night after dinner. Dad was saying he called the hospital on the mainland, and they've got some special doctor visiting from a clinic in Boston. He does plastic surgery on burn victims. Dad said he asked him to examine Jeff's face when he goes in next week to get his walking cast. If he thinks he can do the operation, Dad's going to pay for it."

"Why hasn't anybody consulted me about this?"

"Mother asked Dad not to. She said she didn't think they ought to get your hopes up or Jeff's either. She thought they ought to wait first and see what the doctor said."

"So you decided to jump the gun and break the news yourself?"

"I wanted to see what you'd say."

"What did you expect?"

"I thought maybe you'd say, 'That's great' or something like that."

"It isn't great," Lia said harshly. "They have no right to do this. It's thousands of dollars we're talking about. Without my permission, they're planning to hand away a part of my inheritance!"

"Don't talk like that," Meg said. "You don't inherit things till people die, and Dad and Mother aren't old or sick or anything."

"The time people die isn't always determined by how old they are. People can have accidents."

"Like you and Jeff on the rocks?"

"There are all sorts of accidents. Nobody's immune to them. I don't think Jeff will take the money. He's got too much pride. He'll refuse the offer, especially when he realizes what's behind it."

"I don't know what you mean," Meg said.

"It's a bribe, of course. It's a bribe to keep him out of my life. Our parents are protective. They don't want me hounded day and night by some half-faced freak when I could be going with a guy like Gordon. They're willing to pay off Jeff with plastic surgery or anything else he wants in order to make sure that he leaves me alone."

"They don't have to do that," Meg objected. "Jeff won't call you if he thinks you don't want to see him. He's not like that."

"That's not what our parents think. They know what disturbed people are capable of, and they're afraid for my safety. What's that thing that Rennie says? Mary Beth repeated it to me just yesterday. It's something about Jeff's personality being as messed up as his face."

The ferry horn sounded, cutting through the conversation with three short, imperative blasts.

"We'd better hurry," Meg said with nervous relief. I knew she was upset, not only by the views Lia was expressing, but by the fact that they were coming from a respected older sister.

"You'd better run," agreed Lia. "When you get on board, tell Jeff to get off and wait for me at the end of the pier."

"Tell him to get off? But the boat's getting ready to pull out!"

"You heard me," Lia snapped. "Tell him I need to see him. We can miss school one day without the world's coming to an end. It's more important to get this thing straightened out before Dad gets to him."

"Don't tell him what you just said to me," Meg pleaded. "It'll make him feel terrible. Dad and Mother like Jeff. I know they're not scared for you."

"I'll talk to anyone I want and say what I choose." Lia's voice held a note of command. "Get going! You're going to miss the boat yourself if you stay here arguing. Tell Jeff to get off and wait for me."

The ferry sounded a final warning. Meg shot Lia one last look of bewildered outrage. Then she whirled and took off like a startled rabbit down the snow-covered road.

Lia stood, watching her. She herself was breathing as rapidly as though it were she who was running. Her warm breath made short puffs of steam in the icy air.

"Accidents happen," she repeated softly. "And you, Miss Know-It-All, are first in line to have one. Or, perhaps, you'll be second. Jeff had better not try playing any holdout games. I haven't come this far to lose out now on what should be mine."

She began to walk unhurriedly toward the pier, following the erratic line of the children's footsteps. She was wearing my favorite cap, a bright red one with a tassel. Neal had given it to me for Christmas the year before. Her hands were thrust deep into the pockets of my old ski jacket. The fur-lined boots on her feet were mine; the muffler around her neck was my plaid one with the fringe.

She looked like Laurie. She was dressed in Laurie's clothing. And yet —

I drew ahead so that I could see her approaching as Jeff

242

would see her — a familiar figure, cheeks flushed with cold, eyes squinted against the brilliance of sunlight on snow. Would he be deceived as easily as my family?

Much as I wanted to believe that he would not be, I knew it was doubtful. I could see differences. Lia's walk was not the same as mine — it was more careful, more precise. Although the features were my own, the set of the mouth was not. But these things were too subtle, and Jeff would not be on the alert for them. He would be expecting Laurie, and it would be she whom he would see.

I had not been with Jeff since the day before the storm. I could have, of course, if I had chosen to. I had the ability to go to him at home or at school. I could stand at his shoulder while he did his homework; I could rest beside him when he slept. I had not done these things because I could not bear to. I did not want to see the effect of what Lia had done to him.

The phone call had been short and brutal.

"It was a mistake," she had told him. "I must have been crazy to have let myself get involved with you. Gordon and I have patched things up, and I don't want you bothering me anymore."

I had stood there, helpless, cringing as I listened to the sound of my own voice speaking the incredible words. I knew the hurt they were inflicting, but I was powerless to prevent it.

As I was powerless, now, to stop the thing that was going to happen on the pier.

Jeff, believe her — accept what she tells you — react as she hopes you will! Tell my parents to keep their rotten bribe money!

I hurled the words with all the strength that my mind possessed. Would he sense the message? It was the best I could hope for. If he didn't, there was nothing more I could do to warn him. Jeff was strong, but he was balancing on crutches, and the water at the pier's end was cold and deep.

The ferry was already three hundred yards offshore now, chugging along like some huge, determined water animal. Its decks were empty, so Lia would not have to be concerned about witnesses. Gordon and Nat and the others would be down in the cabin, protected from the wind, laughing and chatting and, perhaps, wondering why Laurie Stratton was skipping school.

"I talked to her last night," Gordon would be saying. "There was nothing wrong with her then. In fact she sounded more like herself than she has in months."

Jeff was waiting at the end of the pier as Lia had requested, slouched over his crutches and looking belligerent. Gone was the good-humored self-confidence of recent weeks. This was the old Jeff Rankin, jaw set defensively, face dark with brooding hostility. I moved toward him as Lia did, watching his eyes narrow with a flicker of some emotion I could not identify.

For a moment neither of them spoke. It was Jeff who broke the silence.

"So, what's up?" His voice was cool and carefully noncaring. "Meg says it's important. Did Ahearn dump you again?"

"You'd like that, wouldn't you?" Lia said. "But I'm afraid it hasn't happened, and there's not much chance it's going to. If it did, I wouldn't be rebounding in your direction. This is something else entirely. It's about my father —" She broke off the sentence, a look of surprise flashing across her face. This was immediately replaced by an expression of such total fury that I could not recognize my own features.

"What are *you* doing here?"

"I wanted to stay with Jeff." Megan stepped out from behind him, her hands extended in a gesture of pacification. Inanely, I wondered what she had found to do with her snowball. "Please, Laurie, don't act like this. Go back like you used to be. I don't *like* you anymore!"

"Do you think that I like you?" Lia snapped. "You're a forty-year-old brain in a fat midget's body! I told you to get on that boat and stay there. It's Jeff I need to talk to."

Meg turned to Jeff. "See what I mean? She's not Laurie anymore! She's mean, like the ghost thing turned solid!"

"Ghosts don't turn solid," Jeff said. "They're things of the spirit. But a practiced one might project so well that she could create a realistic illusion. That would be easy enough to discover. All we'd need to do is grab hold of her."

He reached out so quickly that Lia could not jerk back soon enough to avoid contact. His hand closed upon her arm, and I watched the momentary expression of anticipation fade as he felt the solidity of bone and flesh beneath the padded thickness of the parka.

"Get your hands off me!" snarled Lia. "I mean that! It makes me sick to look at you, much less have you touch me!"

"That's not the song you were singing a couple of weeks ago."

"I told you before, I must have been crazy!"

She drew back her free hand as though she were preparing to strike him, and Jeff released the crutch he was leaning on and made a grab for her wrist.

"She's no ghost, Meg," he said grimly. "Much as I hate to admit it, this is your sister."

245

"It's Laurie on the outside, but inside it's the ghosty! I know it! I can feel it!" Meg was almost hysterical. "She doesn't eat drumsticks! She doesn't remember anything like she ought to! She hates everybody! My real Laurie wasn't like that!"

"I don't know. Is it possible?" He hesitated, his hand still tight around the flailing wrist. "Say, Laurie, remember the day you first came over to my place? You brought the books. It was right after the accident. The radio was blaring, and you told me to turn it down. What was playing? What group was playing?"

"How should I remember? Kansas? Tomboy? One of the rock groups."

"You've got to remember. You made such a big deal about the racket they were making. You wanted to talk, and I was hiding behind the noise. I was scared of what you might be going to say."

"Those bands all sound alike. What difference does it make?"

"None," Jeff said. "Except that it wasn't a band. It wasn't even a radio. There was a western on television with a lot of yelling and shooting. You can't have forgotten that." He released his grip, and she jerked her arm away from him as though she had been burned. His own right hand flew to his pocket. "I brought you something. I was going to give it to you at school today. It's the necklace from Helen. I fixed the clasp."

"I don't want it," Lia told him quickly.

"It's the fetish, the eagle! It's defense against evil spirits from the skies! You were wearing it the first time you projected. Was that why your body stayed safe?" His voice had changed in tone. It was no longer sullen, and his eyes

246

were bright with suspicion. "Are you Laurie? Or can Meg be right after all? Are you her 'ghosty'? Are you *Lia?*"

He pulled the fetish from his pocket and held it high. Lia's eyes focused upon the thin, silver chain with the bright blue bird in its center, and she drew back with a gasp.

"Get that thing away! I told you, I don't want it!"

Her hand whipped out and struck the chain from his fingers. Caught by surprise, Jeff stumbled backward, grabbing out for some kind of support, but his hands closed upon empty air. He struggled frantically to keep his balance as his bad leg went out from under him, and he went down in a sprawled heap.

Instantly, Lia was in motion. Before I could fully take in what was happening, she had caught up one of the fallen crutches and was swinging it above her head like a battle ax. I lifted my voice in a silent scream as I realized her intention.

Megan's cry was an echo of the sound I had not made. Moving with a speed unbelievable for someone so small and plump, she bent and snatched the fallen necklace from the dock where it had landed when Jeff lost his grip on it.

"Go away!" she shrieked. "Bad thing, go away!"

Drawing back her stubby arm, she hurled the fetish straight at Lia.

It struck her solidly across the throat, and in that fraction of a second, something happened. Lia seemed to stop and stagger. The crutch slid from her upraised hand, and as it fell, that hand became my own. Abruptly, the resistance was gone, and I felt the astral cord snap tight with a jerk so powerful that I gasped in pain.

And I heard it — that gasp! It was not silent!

I could speak! I could cry! I could feel!

The freezing air of winter stung my face. My right wrist throbbed at the spot where Jeff's strong fingers had dug into the flesh. I stood, immobile, stunned by the sensations I was experiencing, so long familiar, yet suddenly so new.

"I'm back!" I cried. "I'm home!"

I listened, ecstatic, to the sound of my own voice ringing out triumphantly. Then I pitched forward, laughing and crying like a mad thing, into the haven of Jeff's upraised arms.

So, we have come full cycle. My eighteenth birthday passed during the course of this writing, and it is again September. I have met my self-imposed deadline, and this story is completed.

But, is it? In life there are no real endings or beginnings. Where is the true beginning of this saga? At the moment when I first saw Lia? At our birth? At our conception? Or centuries before that, when the first picture of an astral body, hovering over a physical one, was painted and placed in an Egyptian tomb?

So much is left unanswered. I wonder often about Helen. I received a short, formal note from Mr. Tuttle about a month ago telling me that she was well and would be repeating her senior year at a school on the Shiprock Reservation. She still has no memory of the time they spent in New England. He asked me not to try to contact her.

"There are some things better put behind us," he said.

What lies ahead for Jeff and me? We have not seen each other for months now. In May, Jeff's father remarried, and Jeff himself had surgery at a hospital in Boston. It was successful, though more surgery will be needed. He is staying with his mother until his doctors feel that he is ready for the second operation.

Jeff writes, "I'll never be a pretty boy, but, thanks to your folks, I'll have another crack at looking human."

A new chapter of his life is in the making. Will there be a place in it for me? Or was I meant to play a particular role at a certain time, a girl he loved when other girls would not have him?

And Lia? What of Lia? I know she dwells at Cliff House. I do not see her, but I feel her nearness. At night I hear her, or think I hear her — a stirring of the air by my pillow — a rustle in the hall outside my bedroom door. Faint and soft, in dreams I hear her whisper, *You, Laurie! I blame you!*

What is it that she blames me for? Why does she stay? For what is she waiting? Surely she knows I will not be foolish enough to project myself again. She has a body of her own. Why does she not return to it?

Those were the questions I discussed with Megan. They were answered, surprisingly, by my father.

He came in one night and sat down on the end of my bed.

"I've got some news for you, Laurie," he said. "I'm afraid it will upset you, but I think you ought to hear it. I've been on the phone with Arthur Abbott."

"How did you know about him?" I asked.

"I checked out a long-distance call that turned up on our phone bill. The phone company gave me the number. He and I talked for quite a long time. He told me about your call to him. I haven't shared this with your mother, and I don't intend to."

"What is the news you were talking about?"

"Your twin was ill," Dad said. "Extremely ill."

"I know that already. Mr. Abbott told me."

"She was evidently in the habit of sleeping heavily during periods in the daytime. One afternoon she went to sleep and didn't wake up."

"Didn't wake up?" I repeated. "You can't mean that, Dad. Surely a week later —"

"You don't understand," Dad said gently. "There were no vital signs. There was no breathing, no heartbeat."

"You're the one who doesn't understand," I told him. "Perhaps it seemed that way, but eventually I'm certain she regained consciousness."

"The body was cremated, Laurie," my father told me. "I know how upsetting this must be for you, but I thought you ought to know it so that you'll stop this compulsive search of yours. She's gone. It's over. Please, accept that fact. From what Mr. Abbott told me, she was not a person you would have wanted to know."

Is my father right? Is it really over? How far does light fade? Does it ever completely vanish, or does it linger on, faint and indefinable, forever?

"If there were a mile-high mountain of granite, and once every ten thousand years, a bird flew past and brushed it with a feather —"

I will not think about the subject of eternity.

In one more week, I will be leaving for college. For me, as for Jeff, a new phase of life is starting. That is what I will concentrate on. Life continues, and we all of us keep changing and building, toward what we cannot know.

But for now, not because I mean it, but because I have a writer for a father and know from his example what a manuscript should look like, I will write —

THE END